PENGUIN BOOKS

THE ACCIDENTAL WOMAN

Jonathan Coe was born in Birmingham in 1961. His most recent novel is *The Rain Before It Falls*. He is also the author of *The Accidental Woman*, *A Touch of Love*, *The Dwarves of Death*, *What a Carve Up!*, which won the 1995 John Llewellyn Rhys Prize, *The House of Sleep*, which won the 1998 Prix Médicis Étranger, *The Rotters' Club*, winner of the Everyman Wodehouse Prize, and *The Closed Circle*. His biography of the novelist B.S. Johnson, *Like a Fiery Elephant*, won the 2005 Samuel Johnson Prize for best non-fiction book of the year. He lives in London with his wife and two children.

The Accidental Woman

JONATHAN COE

PENGUIN BOOKS

PENGUIN BOOKS

Published by the Penguin Group
Penguin Books Ltd, 80 Strand, London WC2R 0RL, England
Penguin Group (USA) Inc., 375 Hudson Street, New York, New York 10014, USA
Penguin Group (Canada), 90 Eglinton Avenue East, Suite 700, Toronto, Ontario, Canada M4P 2Y3
(a division of Pearson Penguin Canada Inc.)
Penguin Ireland, 25 St Stephen's Green, Dublin 2, Ireland (a division of Penguin Books Ltd)
Penguin Group (Australia), 250 Camberwell Road, Camberwell, Victoria 3124, Australia
(a division of Pearson Australia Group Pty Ltd)
Penguin Books India Pvt Ltd, 11 Community Centre, Panchsheel Park, New Delhi – 110 017, India
Penguin Group (NZ), 67 Apollo Drive, Rosedale, Auckland 0632, New Zealand
(a division of Pearson New Zealand Ltd)
Penguin Books (South Africa) (Pty) Ltd, 24 Sturdee Avenue,
Rosebank, Johannesburg 2196, South Africa

Penguin Books Ltd, Registered Offices: 80 Strand, London WC2R 0RL, England

www.penguin.com

First published by Gerald Duckworth and Co. Ltd 1987
First published in Penguin Books in 2000
This edition published for The Book People Ltd, 2011
Hall Wood Avenue, Haydock, St Helens, WA11 9UL

1

Copyright © Jonathan Coe, 1987
All rights reserved

Typeset by Intype London Ltd
Printed in England by Clays Ltd, St Ives plc

ISBN 978-0-241-96092-9

www.greenpenguin.co.uk

Penguin Books is committed to a sustainable
future for our business, our readers and our
planet. This book is made from paper certified
by the Forest Stewardship Council.

Contents

I. *Beforewards*

Take a birth. Any birth.

Arriving on the threshold of womanhood (for it is she, as chance would have it) Maria finds herself in Mrs Leadbetter's study. Mrs Leadbetter the headmistress. She beamed at Maria and waved her to an armchair. Outside it was dark.

'I won't keep you long,' she said. 'I wanted to say this only: that we are proud of you, Maria. The first of our girls in fifty-four years to have won a place at Oxford. What an opportunity stretches before you. How excited you must be.'

Maria smiled.

'One doesn't like to crow,' said Mrs Leadbetter, 'but the boys' school this year has secured only three places. Out of twelve entrants, this represents only twenty-five per cent. And yet out of our two entrants, you represent fifty per cent success. You must feel very proud.'

Mrs Leadbetter had a peculiar face, very brown and wrinkled. She was a stout woman. Her breasts resembled nothing so much as two Dundee rock cakes (bonus size) of the sort sold in the bakery just around the corner, although strictly speaking this was a comparison which Mr Leadbetter alone was entitled to draw. Maria anyway took no notice of her, her mind running on the school motto, *Per ardua ad astra*, which she could read, upside down, on Mrs Leadbetter's headed notepaper.

'In less than a year's time, Maria, you will be going to Oxford,' the old woman continued. 'It is a city of dreams. I went there myself, of course. Yes, I can remember doing my Christmas shopping there once. Have you any idea, Maria, what an exciting time of your life approaches? Freed from school's closed world, you fling yourself pell-mell into the giddy whirl of life, in the company of life's gay young things on the doorstep of their dreams.'

Maria did not believe a word of this, of course. She was inexperienced, but not stupid, and in the last few years she had begun to notice things, and to withdraw, unimpressed, from the society of her school friends, her former play-mates. Miserable Maria, they had started to call her. Moody Mary. Childish nicknames, that's all. Shit-face. Snot-bag. Their invention was inexhaustible. Maria's reserve infuriated Mrs Leadbetter, as usual.

'You are a quiet girl, Maria. You have a silent and studious disposition, admirable in one so young. You channel your youthful high spirits into the peaceful streams of the intellect, the passive contemplation of the great works of art and literature. You are placid, imperturbable.'

Maria was thinking furiously of a way to be rid of this maniac. She craved her lamp-lit bedroom.

'All I wanted to say, Maria, is that I and all the staff, all of us here at St Jude's, are behind you and rooting for you, and are pleased and proud with what you have done. We want your time at Oxford to be the glorious start of a life rich in achievement and fulfilment. You must begin even now to prepare yourself for it, psychologically and spiritually. Think daily on your success, Maria, and what it will mean for you. Look forward to it with joy and anticipation. Be thrilled.'

A hard thing to ask, that, of Maria, whom little thrilled, not even the darkness through which she walked that evening on her way to the bus stop. It was a cold night, and school was empty, but for the cleaners to be seen at work in bright windows. The homeward traffic hummed, the chill breeze swept, Maria shivered.

Beneath the street lamp which marked her bus stop she could see that Ronny was waiting for her. She sensed also that it was going either to rain or to snow, soon, perhaps before she had finished her walk up the long hill. She was too tired to feign pleasure on being greeted by him.

'I thought I'd wait for you,' said Ronny. He added, when they were on the top deck of the bus together, driving past the closing shops, the dark offices and factories, 'Just think, a year from now, we will be in Oxford together.'

'Ronny,' said Maria, 'why did you apply to go to Oxford? You told me once that you never wanted to go there.'

'I applied because you will be there.'

'But supposing I hadn't got in, and you had? Where would have been the sense in that? You did a very dangerous thing, Ronny, because you tried to calculate how things would turn out in the future.'

'But I was right.'

'Supposing I were to die before then.'

Here you are to imagine a short silence.

'I love you, Maria.'

'And yet you know that I think you are very foolish. If you think you can control your life in this way, then why don't you find another girl, one who knows what you mean by those words.'

This advice stung Ronny to what we in the trade refer to as the quick. However, he ignored it as usual.

When the bus reached the terminus, they performed a small ritual, as follows. Ronny asked Maria if he could walk her home, Maria refused, Maria descended from the bus, Ronny remained on it, and he then rode all the way back to school and beyond, for his home did not lie in the same direction as Maria's, no. Accompanying Maria on her bus home involved for him a detour of some twenty-three miles, and the loss on a good day of some seventy-four minutes which could have been usefully spent on homework or on indulgence in pop-eyed sexual reverie. He would arrive home horrendously late, to a cold supper, to the wrath of his parents, to the scorn and taunts of his brothers and sisters. But he suffered all this gladly for Maria. So that's two clowns we have met already.

Alighting from her bus, Maria next had to walk up the long hill. Certain preparations were essential. She put down her bag, her bag full of books, and buttoned up her coat, every button, for there was an attempt at snow after all. She turned up her collar, and pulled on her gloves. Now a decision had to be made. There was a café at the bus terminus where Maria could, if she desired, sit and drink a cup of coffee, or of hot chocolate, or could eat a sandwich, sitting in the corner. She had a favourite seat in the corner, and she could see that it was empty. But she decided against it, this evening, because she did not really have the money, and she did not really have the time, and above all she did not really want to, if the truth be told. So she picked up her bag and began to walk, this aged aged schoolgirl, past the café, and past the newspaper shop, past all the shops until there were no more shops, only bare woods on either side of the road, and the occasional house, and the road started to rise and the hill began.

It occurred to Maria, sometimes, as she walked up the hill on dark and frankly cold nights such as this, that there was every chance that one day she might be accosted, and perhaps mugged, and conceivably raped, and then left for dead, for the road was not used much by pedestrians. She did not see what she could very well do about this. She could only get home by climbing the hill, and she was not prepared to stay away from home, in spite of home's obvious drawbacks, for a night away from home, out in the dark without a roof over your head, where is the pleasure in that. Perhaps her parents might have come to the bus terminus, in their car, and have given her a lift home, but the offer had never been made, and it is by no means certain that had it ever been made Maria would ever have accepted it. The whole question is only important insofar as it should be stressed that among Maria's sensations, as she walked up the hill of an evening, was the fear that some day something like that might happen, and she was often afraid, at this time of her life, not very afraid but often very slightly fearful, of what might one day befall her. And it was often in the dark that these fears took shape, although generally speaking she preferred the dark to the light, any day of the week.

In those days Maria wrote poems, too. For instance, she composed a poem, or fragments of a poem, on her walk home that evening. It was a peculiar poem, well worth preserving, I wish I could give you the whole of it. Unfortunately it was destroyed, along with so many other mementoes of Maria's life at this period, in the fire which burnt down half of her parents' home in 1982. (Touching to reflect that of this event, which is not due for nearly twelve years yet, she has at present little inkling.) The poem concerned, among other things, the contact of half-formed snowflakes with unresisting cheek, the act of unthinking uphill progression, the texture of street lamp glow where it merges with winter sky, and the comfort to be derived from states of solitude. Maria felt happiest when she was alone, by and large, but the thought of being always alone terrified her, because she was only human, the source you might say of all her problems. Why Maria wrote these poems, what pleasure she took in wrestling with emotions, disguising them as thoughts and misrepresenting them in words, what satisfaction she derived from copying them out in a fair hand and reading them over to herself, I cannot say. Probably none.

Arriving home, Maria shouted hello to her mother, at work in the kitchen, for she was not averse to showing affection occasionally, and then went straight upstairs to her bedroom, where her brother was practising the violin. He stopped when she came in and they had a short, monosyllabic conversation. Sympathy, understanding, affection, trust, liking and love are all words completely inappropriate to describe the feelings felt by Maria for her brother, and vice versa. Soon he folded his music stand and left, much to Maria's satisfaction. Alone again and inside at last, things were looking up. She deliberated between her bed and her chair, opting finally for the latter as being the more conducive to thought, since she wanted to think. She turned her bedside light on, the other lights off, and, while up, she wondered whether to listen to some music, on her portable cassette player. She decided not, because it was hard to think while listening to music, in her experience, you only ended up wasting one or the other. No, there was no need for music, that evening.

She thought, believe it or not, about Mrs Leadbetter's words. These were what occupied her young mind. They made no sense to her, not surprisingly, but more disturbing than that, Maria could think of no reason for Mrs Leadbetter's having spoken them which made sense to her either. She had a feeling, she had had a feeling in the study that afternoon, that something was expected of her, that now that she had done what had been expected of her, namely, passed her exam, something else was going to be expected of her. It was not simply that she was expected to be pleased with herself for having passed her exam, she was already pleased with herself for having passed the exam, she would not have taken the exam if she had not thought that to pass it would give her pleasure. Rather, her unease had something to do with the peculiar way in which it seemed to be required that she should manifest her pleasure. Maria had never been good at manifesting pleasure, although she was quite capable of feeling it, in her own way. As for excitement, that was quite beyond her, and had been since the age of about seven. So Mrs Leadbetter was really asking the impossible of her. This gave no particular cause for alarm, Maria had never felt any need to do what Mrs Leadbetter asked of her. However, she suspected that it meant that her parents would also ask the impossible of her, and this was more serious, partly because the bearability of domestic life depended to a large extent on the maintenance of good relations with her father and mother, and partly because she still bore towards them the vestiges of a sense of duty, the origins of which she had always chosen, sensibly, not to analyse.

But perhaps we could undertake this analysis for her.

Her gratitude towards her parents centred mainly, unbelievable though this may seem, around some memories for which they were indirectly responsible. Yes,

Maria had happy memories of her childhood, who hasn't. We all have our memories, we hoard them up and shape them to our requirements. We do things simply so that one day, it may be the next, we shall have the pleasure of remembering them, I can't think of any other reason. Yet it is curious, isn't it, there can be few things more useless, for practical purposes, than happy memories, except perhaps hopes, but then I don't want to start getting difficult at this stage. There'll be plenty of time for that later. These memories, anyway, were of events which used to take place on Sunday afternoons, little family excursions, walks and drives, to places of scenic or historic interest. They would climb into the car, the four of them, mother and father and Maria and little Bobby, and they would go to the woods, or to the common, or to the hills, or to a village, or to a museum, or to a garden, or to pick blackberries if it was the blackberry season, or to sit and watch the fishermen if it was the fishing season. Maria regarded these outings as evidence of parental affection, which was reasonable enough, for if her parents had been doing it merely to get the children out of the house, then they would not have come with them, but would have sent them out alone, or with an aunt or an uncle, and if they had merely wanted to get out of the house them-selves, then they would have left the children behind, under the care perhaps of their grandparents. This affec-tion seemed all the stranger, too, when she considered that as children she and Bobby had been, to put it mildly, insufferable, and much prone to fighting, and shouting, and biting, and screaming, and peeing, and puking. There was one Sunday afternoon which she remembered with particular fondness. She remembered it even now, this evening, in her bedroom chair. They had gone to the park, they called it the park, it was a ragged construct of meadow, trees, gorse, hawthorn, stretching over a hill or two five miles from home, with a fine view, for those who like that sort of thing, of the countryside, in one direction, and of Birmingham, in the other, and not far from the motorway, that was its real attraction, so that it was never quiet up there, you could always hear the roar of the traffic as well as the singing of birds, the mooing of cows, and all the other country noises which are so nice, if that sort of stuff appeals to you. The park. It was here one Sunday afternoon that Maria and her family were separated, by chance, for ten minutes at the most, but to Maria it seemed longer, much longer. She can only have been seven or eight. How she cried, and ran, and wandered, tearing her socks on the brambles and falling, in the end, so hard that she could not get up, and how they had called, Maria! Maria!, further and nearer, further and nearer. It was the crying finally drew them to her. Meanwhile a man had found her, he had come across her in the grass. Hello, little girl, he had said, why are you crying, or words to that effect, he had asked some bloody stupid question anyway, she remembered that much. In retrospect he had probably been going to molest her, this thought had not occurred to Maria at the time. But at that moment Bobby found her, he had heard the sobs, and then her mother was stooping to cradle her and brushing away the tears with the arm of her rough tweed overcoat, and Maria, although she did not stop crying for a good while yet, had never known joy like it, before or since.

Maria sustained her affection for her parents on the basis of memories such as this.

The point being, that they did not yet know of her success in the examination. Maria herself had only found out, from Mrs Eccles, that very afternoon. The news could not fail to give them pleasure, but by the same token, her own response to it could not fail to give them pain. Maria wondered why this should be so. She herself was glad to be going to Oxford next year, it seemed to her as good a thing to do next year as any. On the other hand there was no reason to suppose that she would enjoy being at Oxford, any more than she enjoyed being at school, and Maria was opposed to the idea of being pleased or excited without reason. So how to break the news to her mother and father, in a manner which would not upset or annoy them?

At this point a cat wandered into her bedroom (it was all go in this household, as you can see). This creature, a small brown and white tabby called Sefton, was only two years old but had a bearing and a philosophy of life which belied his age. Maria genuinely loved him, with a love founded, as it should be, on a profound respect. Sefton seemed to her to have got life sorted out, from top to bottom. The goals of his existence were few, and all admirable: to feed himself, to keep himself clean, and above all to sleep. Maria sometimes believed that she too might be happy, if only she were allowed to confine herself to these three spheres of endeavour. Also, she admired Sefton's attitude towards physical affection. He was for it, from all comers. Perfect strangers had only to stop, to stoop down and to offer him the simplest caress between the ears, and then for a few minutes they would be all over each other, stroking and fondling and rubbing like two young lovers out on the golf course in the throes of pubescent rapture. This was to Maria a source of great envy. Not that she would have liked to be stroked and fondled and rubbed by perfect strangers, of course not. Exactly. What she envied was the fact that Sefton could indulge in this delightful intimacy safe in the knowledge that the pleasure taken in it by himself and his partner was entirely innocent, unless by some misfortune it turned out to be someone of bestial tendencies, and that had never happened to him yet. Not so with Maria. She had, let's not be shy about this, had physical contact with men, or rather boys, before now, although only two, admittedly, on anything like a sustained basis. For she was not averse, at this stage, to the odd kiss, or the odd cuddle, or the occasional orgasm. But more and more she began to see the sexual cravings of the human race, including her own, as the symptom of a far greater craving, a terrible loneliness, an urge for self-forgetfulness which, so the story went, could only be attained in that peculiar private act which tends to take place upstairs, between consenting adults, and with the curtains drawn. She would not have minded touching Ronny, for instance, huddling together on the back seat of the bus, entering preciously for a moment into a shared world, were it not that she suspected his hands would shortly start moving towards her breasts, or diving between her thighs, making with killer instinct for those parts of her which boys always seemed to find so inexplicably interesting. Yes, she would have been partial to men, perhaps she might even have confined herself to one man in particular, if only she had been able to find one who shared her view that intimacy between two people was of value irrespective of whether it led to sticky conflux. But these problems did not exist, you see, for Sefton, and not only in his dealings with men and women, but also in his dealings with other cats, for he had been thoughtfully neutered, at an early age.

Maria envied Sefton on three counts. The third was this, that nobody ever expected him to take the slightest interest or satisfaction in human affairs. Thus he was at liberty to parade a breathtaking and perfectly legitimate indifference. Just watching him did Maria a power of good, in this respect. He patently didn't give a toss about the family's welfare, except when it affected his own. He was totally self-absorbed, and yet totally unselfish, a condition which Maria knew, already to her great sadness, to be quite unavailable to her. It made him nevertheless her favourite confidant. She could tell him, for example, of her success, without embarrassment, simply because there would be no danger of his displaying the least excitement. Many were the secrets which Maria had told Sefton, because she knew that they would mean nothing to him, and many were the little items of news which she had tried out on him, in order to gain strength from the astonishing nonchalance with which he would hear and ignore them. Every family should keep a cat, for this very reason.

She sat with Sefton on her lap, talking to him of this and that, while he slept, her day at school, her hopes and fears, her quiet desires, until her father returned from work and she was called down to dinner. The family ate dinner in the kitchen. Maria's mother had heated up four pies, which she served with mashed potato and tomato ketchup. Her father consumed his food noisily, trailing his tie in the gravy, while her brother sat withdrawn, too shy and unhappy even to speak. He took small and regular mouthfuls. Maria waited until the meal was half eaten before telling them.

'Mother, I have some news,' she said.

They laid down their forks in unison.

'I passed the exam. I will be going to Oxford next year.'

Here you are to imagine a short scene of family jubilation, I'm buggered if I can describe one.

Her father congratulated her, and praised her cleverness.

Her mother said that it was wonderful news, and told her that she must be very excited.

Her brother remained silent, but grinned.

'You will never look back now, darling,' her mother

continued. 'This is the very opportunity that your father and I never had. Once you have had an education like that, nothing in life will ever be denied to you.'

'You must work hard, and enjoy yourself,' said her father. 'Work hard, and enjoy yourself, and you can't go wrong.'

Her mother wanted to know if anyone else from the school would be going.

'No girls. Three of the boys. Ronny passed too.'

'Ronny will be there! How nice. You know, Maria, I'm sure that boy is very fond of you, and you could find a much worse husband, I'm sure of that.'

'The girl's only seventeen,' said her father, 'and you talk of marriage.'

'Eighteen,' said Maria.

'Let her enjoy herself,' said her father, 'while she is in the full flush of youth. There'll be plenty of time to think of marriage when she *gets* to Oxford.'

'Ronny is such a nice boy,' said her mother, 'he has such nice manners, and he looks so smart in that nice school uniform, and if you ask me it is only a matter of time before those boils disappear altogether.'

Maria's father now rose from his chair, advanced towards Maria, and kissed her on the forehead. He had done nothing like it for a matter of weeks, perhaps months. She gave a faint and not entirely forced smile.

'We must celebrate,' he said. 'Why don't I go out to the off licence and buy us all a bottle of cider. Or we could go out to the pictures. And then at the weekend we shall go into town together and buy you a nice present. What do you say, Maria?'

But once the initial flurry had subsided, it turned out to be an evening like any other. Bobby was the first to leave the table, for his family frightened him and he could not wait to escape upstairs, where solitary, secret pleasures awaited him. Following his departure, there was a long silence.

'I have homework to do,' said Maria.

'We must not stop the girl doing her homework,' said her father, 'however proud we are of her.'

He started to do the washing up.

Maria, meanwhile, sat in her room, thinking, dreaming, waiting. It was a winter's night like any other. From downstairs she heard the noise of the television, from outside she heard the bare branches of the rose bush as they tapped against her window. Sometimes she drew back the curtain and looked out, at the passing headlights, and at the road which would grow frosty, and at the stars, or, if they intervened, the clouds.

This was typical of the ways in which Maria and her family would spend their evenings, at this period.

2. *The World of Meaningful Looks*

When Maria came to look back on her days at Oxford, which, to her credit, she did very seldom, it seemed to her that it had all taken place in bright sunshine. We can safely assume, I think, that this was in reality not the case, but then who said our concern was with reality, or hers, for that matter. If Maria's memories were of an Oxford bathed in sunlight, we might as well respect them, except perhaps for parts of the third chapter, where the mood will be rather more autumnal. All this is just to give you an idea of how things are likely to turn out. It was in any case autumn by the time she got there, bright blue autumn, and Maria's college, we won't name names, looked very pretty, even to her. She found that she was required to share a room, or rather a set of rooms, with a girl called Charlotte. She would have preferred to have a room to herself. That first evening, they sat together by the fire, and talked long into the night. This gave rise to a spontaneous and mutual antipathy.

'My friends call me Charlie,' Charlotte said. 'What do your friends call you?'

'Maria.'

Eventually the conversation came to a halting conclusion. There was a long silence, which Charlotte was the first to infringe.

'Do you believe, Maria,' she said, 'that there is a certain sort of silence between people, where no words are necessary, and which signals not the end but the start of understanding?'

'Yes,' said Maria, and added to herself, This isn't it.

'Do you believe, Maria,' said Charlotte, after a few more minutes, 'that there is a kind of look which passes between people, and which can speak more than a thousand words and yet still leave so much unsaid?'

'Yes,' said Maria, looking away.

'So much is spoken when people look at one another. Looks are so meaningful. Do you know what I intend to study at Oxford, Maria?'

'Chinese?'

'I mean apart from that. People. One can learn so much about people from the way they look at one another. And do you know what? I shall teach you, Maria. I shall teach you how to study people, and how to learn, from their looks, from their smiles, from what they say to each other and what they leave unsaid. We shall study these things together.'

This, Maria soon realized, was Charlotte's way of admitting that she was morbidly addicted to gossip.

A few weeks passed, as weeks do, try as you may. Maria and Charlotte began to make friends, in and out of college. But Charlotte made considerably more friends than Maria did. Maria did not find it easy to make friends. Also she found friendship a difficult phenomenon to grasp, conceptually. For instance, she was friendly for a while with a girl called Louise, but their friendship did not last long, and while it lasted it was a lukewarm affair, so lukewarm that friendship is frankly too strong a word for it. Maria and Louise attended lectures together, and seminars together, and were united by the similarity of their tastes in literature, in particular their indifference towards the works of Geoffrey Chaucer, their lack of enthusiasm for the poems of Robert Henryson, and their loathing of the writings of Thomas Malory. (All the same, Maria sometimes felt, in private moments, that Louise's indifference was only skin deep.) Sometimes, after a seminar, or a lecture, Louise would accompany Maria back to her rooms, and there they would sit, and talk, and perhaps eat, and then Louise would go, and Maria would find herself thinking, So what? And occasionally, Maria would be walking past Louise's college, and would think to herself, This is where Louise lives, and, having nothing better to do, having nothing to do at all most of the time, she would visit her. Then they would talk, and sit, and perhaps drink, until the time came for Maria to get up and leave, having nothing better to do, and then as she walked back to her rooms she would find herself thinking, Well, what was the point of that, exactly?

Charlotte's friends were a different matter altogether, there is really no point of comparison. They were a noisy crowd, frequently arriving in groups of four or five and staying until tea, dinner, supper or even bedtime.

Charlotte's best friends called on her daily, and if they could not call on her, they telephoned, for Charlotte, without consulting Maria, had installed a telephone in their sitting room. Maria had nothing against telephones per se, she could take them or leave them, but she was inconvenienced by this one because it meant that Ronny had a new means of contacting her. Ronny was at Balliol. Before the telephone was installed, he had been content to call on Maria every day, or simply to send her something, such as some flowers, which she would put in the sitting room, or some chocolates, which she would give to Charlotte, or his love, which was of no use to anyone. Now, however, he would phone at least once in the morning, and at least twice in the afternoon, and at least seven times in the evening, forever inviting Maria to parties, to concerts, to films, to plays, to dinner.

'You're very cruel to that boy, Maria,' Charlotte said one evening, watching her replace the receiver.

'As a matter of fact I like him,' said Maria. 'If he was prepared to be friends with me, that would be all right, but he insists on talking about love all the time.'

'That's not his fault,' said Charlotte. 'Do you know what, I think he has a soft spot for you.'

This is a typical example of her skills at character analysis. It was received with noises of approval by Charlotte's friends, of whom there were three in attendance.

'But perhaps Maria has a soft spot for somebody else, and isn't letting on.'

Giggles ensued.

'Come on, Maria, who is it?'

'There is nobody,' she said.

The conversation turned to the subject of the men for whom those present had spots of various degrees of softness.

'Philip is very handsome, except that his ears are so small.'

'John is quite nice, except that his eyebrows meet in the middle.'

'Maurice is lovely, except for that extra finger on his right hand.'

But Charlotte, at first, had almost as little time as Maria for these concerns. She was not romantic by nature. She was far more interested in the progress of her relationship with her tutor, a woman in her thirties whose destiny, Charlotte had decided, was inextricably bound up with her own.

'I had a very exciting conversation with Miss Ballsbridge this afternoon, Maria,' she confided one night.

'Oh? What did you talk about?'

'It was about ordering some new socks for the hockey team. But it wasn't the *words* which were exciting. It was the looks. We exchanged some very meaningful looks. For instance, at one point I thought to myself, Charlotte, this has gone far enough, no more pussyfooting. So I gave her a look which said, Miss Ballsbridge, I think you know that I think the paths of our lives are destined to run as one. And she replied with a look which I could have sworn was meant to say, Charlotte, I feel, and think that you feel, and feel that you think I feel, a strange closeness for which these words are only a mask. It was a moment charged with feeling. I was about to give her a look which said, Miss Ballsbridge, I'm game if you are, but then we were interrupted, and the chance never arose. She's such a wonderful woman, Maria. I feel that if she were to guide me through life, if I was to guide her, everything would be so wonderful. Life would simply light up, do you know what I mean? Do you ever wish that your life would light up?'

'Sometimes. There's no point in wishing, though.'

Maria knelt down to turn on the gas fire.

Charlotte said suddenly, 'Do you like my friends, Maria?'

'Yes, I do.' (This was almost a lie. But she bore them no malice, at least.) 'Why?'

'I don't know. I just wondered. Sometimes I don't think you do. And then sometimes I do think you do. And then sometimes I don't know whether you do or you don't. Do you want to know whether they like you?'

Maria was unable to answer this question.

'Well, some of them do, and some of them don't,' said Charlotte happily. 'Harriet, for example, doesn't, but Judith does. Harriet thinks you're peculiar. She thinks you have a sinister chin.'

Maria was appalled.

'Harriet wouldn't want you to tell me that,' she said.

'I think that people ought to be told what other people think of them. Just because people tell people things about other people which they don't want them to know, doesn't mean that people shouldn't tell them. Anyway, Alison dislikes you much more than Harriet does.'

'Alison is entitled to her opinion. She is also entitled to have her confidences respected.'

'She thinks you're weird. She asked me if you'd ever been in an institution or had experiments performed on you or anything. I said I didn't know.'

'Charlotte, you shouldn't be telling me these things.'

'So it's not surprising that you don't like them, really. Although I don't see why you shouldn't like Judith, since she likes you so much. She thinks you have an attractive personality. Those were her very words. I'll tell you what I like about Maria. I'll tell you what attracts me to her. It's her personality. With some people, it's because they look nice, or they've got a sense of humour, but with Maria it's her personality. I don't know whether that means she thinks you don't look nice, or haven't got a sense of humour, although Harriet and Alison think both of those things. But anyway, she does like you, an awful lot.' She paused. 'I think Judith is my least favourite of all my friends. But then it's a long time since I drew up a list.'

Maria did not answer. Charlotte got up, stooped beside her and kissed her on the cheek.

'You are sweet,' she said.

Sometimes Charlotte chose to confide in Maria, sometimes she did not: it varied. Maria did not much mind either way. She found it difficult to understand Charlotte.

What she learnt of her affairs, she learnt in fragments, and not in small fragments, let fall frequently, but in irregular fragments, for Charlotte would, perhaps, one night talk of herself incessantly for five and a half hours, and then she would say nothing about herself for a week, or perhaps two. And if Charlotte said nothing about herself, by the way, then you can take it as read that she said nothing at all. So Maria received a very confused impression of Charlotte's affairs, and activities, and daily doings, during the year in which they lived together.

She observed, however, that the paths of Charlotte's and Miss Ballsbridge's lives did not, all hopes notwithstanding, turn out to run as one, but ran parallel for a while and then started to diverge dramatically. Charlotte noticed this too. One day she knocked on Maria's bedroom door, entered, and sat on the bed, so heavily that the act amounted to a gesture of dejection. A sigh would have served the same purpose.

'All is not well,' she said, 'between me and Miss Ballsbridge.'

'I'm sorry to hear that,' said Maria. It was extraordinary how even the most casual conversations seemed to oblige her to say things which were not strictly true.

'We no longer understand each other as we did. Our conversations, once so frequent and so full, are now reduced to cryptic encounters on the quadrangle as we walk to dinner. Our eyes hardly meet. We speak in furtive glances. What do you think of this?'

She handed Maria a sheet of paper, torn from an

exercise pad. It was headed, *Things to put in my look today.*
Maria looked up. Charlotte's eyes were on her earnestly.
This is what she had written:

1. Reproach, but without blame.
2. A sense of hope, poignant and unaffected, perhaps with an intimation of distant joy.
3. Love.
4. A sort of regret that is not despair, tinged with an acknowledgement of the ultimate benevolence of fate, speaking of the knowledge of all that might have been between us, and holding implicit in that knowledge the fragile belief that all might yet be regained.
5. An aura of divine cheerfulness, almost resembling melancholy in its immovability, but which centres on an awareness of the existence of a communion of spirits beyond any which is feasible between two individuals on earth, and which therefore contains and conveys a premonition of this communion while recognizing with calm longing that in the bitter experience of Miss Ballsbridge and myself it was to be felt only in glimpses. Ergo,
6. A farewell pregnant with tones of greeting.

Maria read this through several times.
'This is going to be some look,' she said.
Charlotte nodded.
'How long do you get, normally?'

'Not long. A few seconds.'

She handed back the paper.

'Would you like to try it out on me first?'

'Thank you, Maria, but no. Looks are a private language. It must be to her, and her alone. It would be like talking Greek to a Chinaman.'

Maria never found out whether the look had had the desired effect, so she assumed that it had gone badly. Anyway, Charlotte soon found another object for her affections, a man called Philip, to whom reference has already been made, on account of the smallness of his ears. They had a turbulent affair which lasted for most of the year. Their friendship was entirely Platonic, except that occasionally, rabid with sexual hunger, they would withdraw into the bedroom and thrash about for hours at a time as if their lives depended on it. When this happened Maria, if she was in, would go to her room and read a book. She found the sounds ugly. In those days it was, of course, forbidden for ladies to entertain gentlemen in their rooms at night, so that fornication had to take place during the daytime, an admirable arrangement, it meant that nobody went short of sleep. The course of Charlotte's love for Philip ran fairly smooth at first, but this did not lead Maria to believe even for a moment that it was true. After a few months they ran into difficulties. Maria, dealing with fragments as usual, gathered something to the effect that Charlotte had learnt, at a party, that Philip had spoken of her, at another party, in terms of disrespect, to a third party, whose relaying of the information to a fourth party, at a fifth party, was the channel through which Charlotte had come to hear of it. This merely confirmed, in Maria's opinion, the perniciousness of one of Charlotte's dogmas, which stated that any personal remark was wasted unless it found its way, by however indirect a route, back to the ears of the person about whom it had been made. It transpired, following this incident, that Charlotte and Philip were no longer on speaking terms. They continued to communicate with one another, naturally, but only by means of a complex chain of intermediaries of which Maria, unwillingly, found herself to be part. In performing this function she was expected to deal with nuances of feeling, and of speech, and of interpretation, which were, like MacCruiskeen's chests, so small as to challenge the belief that they really existed. A conventional opening of Charlotte's, for example, would be to say:

'He doesn't love me any more.'

'That's not true,' Maria might counter, with a sinking feeling. 'Only a few hours ago he was here saying that he *did* love you.'

'Ah, but did you notice his tone?'

'I noticed nothing about his tone.'

'Well, Judith said that she thought his *tone* suggested that he was only saying it to give himself time to think of a way of changing the subject. Besides, what about his inflection?'

'What?'

'Didn't you notice that he gave it a sarcastic inflection?

27

Or at least, if not sarcastic, then at least slightly suspicious of the connotations of his own words? Or at least, if not slightly suspicious of the connotations of his own words, then at best half aware that in saying them he was covertly admitting to himself that out of context they had no truth which wasn't questionable at least on a semi-objective level?'

'Judith noticed all this?'

'No. Judith told me that she thought he loved me. But you see, it was the *way* she said it.'

Judith had made considerable advances since those early days, and was now high on Charlotte's list of friends. In the meantime, though, she had decided that she didn't like Maria after all, particularly in respect of her personality. She believed that Maria's grasp of social relations could only be described, in all kindness, as crude. Furthermore, Maria knew that she believed this, because Charlotte had told her so. Judith was skilled in the delicacies out of which her social fabric was woven, and upon which Charlotte's love for Philip was founded. She understood the tone which belied the word, the looks resonant with meaning.

'Have you seen him?' Charlotte would ask her, whenever she called.

'Yes.'

'What did he say about last night?'

Maria would listen.

'Well, he said that he thought your behaviour called for some sort of explanation.'

'Oh? In what way?'

'He thought that you implied he'd given the impression of having thought you were being rude.'

'He said I'd been rude?'

'Well, he implied that you'd been rude by implication.'

'How can I have been rude by implication when any attempt to be more explicit would have been insensitive by definition? Did he mean that if I'd said what he wanted me to say, instead of leaving it unsaid, he wouldn't have known what to say? Is that what he said?'

'Well, that's what he insinuated.'

Things went steadily downhill. Charlotte's and Philip's grisly attempts to sustain some sort of fondness for each other became a topic of general conversation.

'I feel so cheap,' Charlotte said. 'My love isn't my own any more. Everybody talks about it. It's become a spectator sport.'

'I know how you feel,' Judith insisted. 'I understand. That must be the worst of it. I was saying so only the other day, to Harriet, in the Lamb and Flag. I said to her, Poor Charlie, to have her emotions paraded about in public like this. And then Joanna, who was sitting at the next table, leant across, and said, Yes, fancy having everybody gossiping about it, and then even the barman, who was collecting the glasses, said, Charlie? Is that your friend with the dark brown hair, well fancy that, he said, how awful for her.'

'Did he say that? That was kind of him.'

It was Philip that Maria felt sorry for. Not that she felt

very sorry, even for him, for he was a bit of a fool, by anybody's standards, especially hers. But she felt slightly sorry for him because he seemed to be suffering more than anyone else. The day it ended, the day it finally ended, he was in her bedroom, sitting on the bed, his head in his hands. Maria was at her desk, trying to work, but she did not mind, especially. Charlotte was in her own bedroom, sobbing on Judith's shoulder.

'Love destroys,' said Philip, from between his fingers. 'It is a raging fire which warms you, then burns, then leaves you for a heap of ashes, grey and barely glowing.' He got up suddenly. 'Do you mind if I write that down?'

Maria handed him pencil and paper. He stared at his own reflection in her mirror.

'Look at me,' he said. 'I'm a wreck.'

There was no denying it.

'Cheer up,' she said, without looking round.

'Somehow . . . out of these ruins . . .' his voice took on a more determined note, 'I am going to build myself anew.'

'That's the spirit,' said Maria, reaching for her ruler.

'A new life. A new . . . attitude towards life. Yes, that's it.' He peered more closely at the mirror. 'And I think I know how to start. I think I know where the change will have to be made. I shall grow . . . a moustache.'

Maria left him to it, walked out into the sunlight. Bright blue summer. She walked into town, jostled with the shoppers, gazed at the buildings, sat in a café, tried to feel part of a crowd. It didn't work. She heard the noises, distinguished the words, saw the faces, but at a distance, even now at a great distance. Alone. Alone, she left the café and walked towards Magdalen bridge. Light played on the water, shot it through with a cleaner green, light lit up her hair as she began her slow return. She trailed, conscious all around her of beauty, fond of the warm and pleased by the sense of a day already on the wane. A tremor of gladness, that's all, hardly noticed, and hardly to be trusted, for she had only her own word for it, alone.

3. Two Companions

Next year Maria was given a room to herself, which was a relief, by now. It meant that she could stand undisturbed at the window and watch the greyness thicken into black. The leaves, and then the lights. She saw very little of Charlotte. Their paths crossed, occasionally, as paths do, try as you may, and at first Maria was worried lest their sudden meetings should each and always begin on a note of private panic, those little frantic moments of rehearsal, followed by the heavy cheerful hello, delivered to the earth. But Charlotte, it soon became clear, did not want to say hello to her any more, which suited Maria, down to the ground.

There were six rooms on her landing. She was expected to share a bathroom and a lavatory with her neighbours, which she did not mind, because after all such arrangements, whatever their other drawbacks, rarely involve the bathroom or the lavatory being occupied by more than one user at a time. The kitchen was another matter. She was also expected to share the kitchen, and this of course was out of the question. And yet to be certain of having the kitchen to herself, she would have had to cook her meal at a ridiculous hour, at midnight for example, which as it happens is exactly what she got into the habit of doing. And even then, she was not always alone, for Maria had in those days a friend, a new friend. Of her five neighbours, four were the usual harmless lunatics, but one was a girl called Sarah, and in her Maria found something very like a sympathetic spirit, for her she felt something bloody close to friendship, if the truth be told. And so they would do things together sometimes, they came to each other's rooms, and talked, and Maria found herself asking, on these occasions, the question So what? far less often than she had in the days when she used to be friendly with Louise.

On grey afternoons Maria would go to Sarah's room, or Sarah would come to Maria's room, and they would pass the time together, perhaps in silence. For there is not much to talk about, even between friends. Sometimes they would listen to music together, on the radio or on the record player, drinking tea, or they would read together, in silence. It was a happy time. Maria would look back on it, very occasionally, at a great distance, and think of how happy she had been then, slightly exaggerating of course, and she would feel a small shudder take place inside her, not unrelated to fear, and not unrelated to those other emotions which produce tears. There is nothing more miserable than the memory of happiness, a position which can be held from various standpoints, as will be shown in some of the following chapters. By the same token, or do I mean the opposite token, there is nothing more pleasurable than the anticipation of happiness, and when I say nothing, I do not use the word lightly. For happiness itself, it seemed to Maria, had very little meaning in relation to the time spent either looking forward to it or remembering it. Furthermore the actual experience of it seemed entirely unconnected with the experience of anticipating or recollecting it. She never said to herself, when happy, 'This is happiness', and so never recognized it as such when it was taking place. But this did not stop her from thinking, when it was not taking place, that she had a very clear idea of what it was. The truth is that Maria was only really happy when she was thinking of happiness to come, and she was not I think alone in this absurd outlook. It is for some reason far nicer to feel bored, or indifferent, or unexcited, and to think, In a few minutes from now, or a few days, or weeks, I shall be happy, than to be happy and to know, even if not consciously, that the next emotional shift will be away from happiness. Maria had observed many striking examples of this phenomenon. For instance, once, when she and Louise had been friends, they had agreed to go to the theatre together. Maria made the arrangements, and offered to buy the tickets, and when the matter was settled, Louise had said, with a joyful smile (she was easily pleased, it's no wonder she and Maria never got on that well), 'I shall look forward to it'. Those were her very words. And to Maria, as she walked back to her room, they suddenly seemed to be quite extraordinary. She realized that Louise had just expressed pleasure at the anticipation of the anticipation of pleasure. And she realized, moreover, that this was by no means uncommon.

She had heard people say, 'I shall look forward to that', or, 'I am going to look forward to that', just as often, if not more often, than she had heard them say, 'I am looking forward to that'. This could not, in her opinion, be unintentional. In fact, she was fully prepared to believe that what they really looked forward to was not the event itself, the supposed object of the anticipation, such as a visit to the theatre, but the very anticipation, no less, those pleasurable hours, or days, or weeks, of hopeful looking forward, during which the mind's eye had some cheering goal to set itself on. And it seemed to Maria, once she had realized this, that the scope for perniciousness inherent in this arrangement was infinite.

So by now Maria was fully aware of what she was doing when, while walking home from a lecture, say, she set her eyes on Sarah's window and felt a glow of comfort at the thought that in only a few minutes she would be sitting with her friend in the warmth, a mug of tea between her hands, the hiss of the gas fire the only accompaniment to their broken conversation. She knew full well that this glow of comfort was in itself far nicer than anything which her friend's room held in store for her. She knew this for a fact, but she persisted, and who can blame her.

Not that Maria's and Sarah's friendship comprised nothing more than sitting together in each other's rooms, or cooking spaghetti bolognese in enormous proportions at midnight, or consuming huge quantities of lasagne at one o'clock in the morning. It was not confined to indoor activities, by any means. For if there was one thing that they both enjoyed, it was the fresh air, provided that it was not too cold outside, or too warm. In particular they favoured the University Parks, since these were not too far from home. It is impossible to analyse the pleasure they derived from these walks, except to say that it was acute, and that because they themselves could never really understand, or picture, this pleasure, then the actual experience of it seemed, for once, far to outweigh any pleasure to be derived from anticipating it. Furthermore, at an hour's or a day's distance, Maria would sometimes look back on her most recent walk with pleasure, which is surely little short of miraculous, although implicit in her pleasure, perhaps, was the thought that another equally pleasurable walk was just around the corner. These walks, to sum up, offered pleasure of a different complexion from any that Maria had known before, a very different complexion.

However, a distinction should be drawn between Maria and Sarah simply walking together, and Maria and Sarah walking together and, simultaneously, talking. The latter was a very different process and offered pleasure of a less unalloyed sort, although of course if they recognized this, and it is by no means certain that they did, it did not stop them from talking to each other, for people always want to talk to each other, even friends, for some reason. When Maria and Sarah walked they did so, needless to say, arm in arm, their bodies pressed gently together, whether it was cold or not, but especially if it was cold. This enabled them to regard their separation, their involuntary and inevitable separation, from the rest of the world, from the park, from the trees, above all from the other walkers, not with unease but with joy, for what did it matter, while they were together, while they were close? It only heightened their closeness, it only meant that they felt their togetherness more keenly. Through the contact of their bodies, or rather their coats, through the linking of their arms, or rather their sleeves, they moulded into one another, they blended as one. But their voices, when they spoke, rarely had the same effect. The soul, assuming that such a thing exists, seeks to find expression in various ways, none of which are terribly satisfactory: in silences, in looks (Charlotte would have agreed with all this), in sounds, but above all in words. Maria and Sarah talked, therefore, as friends do, with a view to achieving a touching and entwining of souls, just as their bodies, when they walked, touched and entwined. But it very rarely came off, it has to be admitted. This is not to say that they ever disagreed, or quarrelled, or misunderstood each other, or at least not very often. But whether it was because words are tricky little bastards, and very rarely say what you want them to say, or because Maria's and Sarah's souls were not cut out for each other in the way that their bodies were (for most people's bodies are cut out for most other people's bodies, when it comes to the crunch), they never felt, when they talked together, as close as when they walked together and did not talk together. Yet still, as I said before, this did not prevent them from talking together, or indeed from doing so with enjoyment, of a sort.

Picture if you can a day in late autumn, or early winter, if you prefer. It is early evening, or late afternoon, if you'd rather. In a distant corner of the park, nearest to Maria's college, there is an ornamental pond, made up of lilies, and reeds, and algae, and of course water, a nice enough mess in all. This was where, and this was when, Maria and Sarah most liked to walk, and sit, and talk.

'You alarm me, Maria,' Sarah said, on one such occasion.

Maria smiled fondly. 'Why?'

'Because nothing excites you. Nothing amuses you. Nothing moves you.'

'That's not true.'

'Sometimes I think you're unhappy.'

'Sometimes I am unhappy. But not now. I'm no more unhappy than you, or than any other girl, really.'

'Do you know who I feel sorry for?' Sarah asked. 'Any man who falls in love with you.'

Maria laughed. 'Men don't know what love is.'

'Neither do you, Maria. You've never been in love, have you?'

'I know what love isn't. It's none of the things people tell us it is.' Then it occurred to her to ask, 'Why, have you been in love?'

'I think so.'

'Tell me about love.'

Sarah said nothing at first. 'I can't tell you. It can't be described.'

'Does it hurt?'

'Yes.'

'Is it worth it?'

'Yes.'

'How does it hurt?'

'You feel very empty and confused. Like trying to catch the wind, in a butterfly net. For the first time in your life you know exactly what you want. You spend every day looking for it. Then it comes, for an instant, and then it's gone. Then it comes again. When you're with . . . whoever it is you love . . . then you're happy . . . nearly always . . . at first.'

'Then it is worth it?'

'Yes.'

'"There are moments in life worth purchasing with worlds". Do you believe that?'

'Yes, I suppose I do believe something like that. And you don't, Maria, you see, you don't believe anything like that at all. Doesn't it make you want to believe it, that I do?'

Maria did not answer.

'That's what worries me. That's what makes me wonder whether you'll ever be happy. That's what makes me wonder whether you'll ever get married.'

'Explain the train of thought,' said Maria, 'which leads from love, to happiness, and then to marriage.'

'Cynicism doesn't suit you, Maria. Don't be cynical.'

'It's you who are cynical. Surely, when so many marriages end in ugliness or unhappiness, it would be cynical to believe that they were ever founded on love. That would be to admit that love has no power to hold people together. Far better to say that there never was any love, and that when a marriage ends, it is simply an economic contract that has been broken.'

'One day,' said Sarah, 'you will unsay all that. One day, when you are married, you will look back on today and think what a foolish girl you were to say all these things.'

Maria did not answer.

'You have such a loving nature, Maria, that's what amazes me. You love to love people, don't you?'

'Of course. But I know so few lovable people.'

'Your standards are too high.'

'It's not standards. I can't help it when I don't understand people.'

'Fall in love, Maria.'

Maria laughed, or cried, I forget which. Sarah took Maria in her arms and they sat, very quiet, for only a few seconds.

'No. Don't fall in love. I don't want you ever to love anyone but me. I want you, all to myself.'

*

Unfortunately for Sarah, for both of them in fact, and surprisingly, too, Maria did not heed this advice, the most heartfelt she had ever been given. Not that she instantly fell in love, strictly speaking, but she had a try. The man in question was called Nigel. He was a friend of Ronny's.

It was at about this time that Ronny got into the habit of proposing marriage to her, and so it must also have been at about this time that she got into the habit of refusing him. These proposals were never especially dramatic, that was something to be thankful for, they simply arose in the normal course of conversation. Ronny never went down on his knees, for instance, because he had a keen sense of his own dignity, and his proposals were always made in a public place, for Maria never went to his room, and always found excuses for not inviting him to hers. Nevertheless he seemed to mean it, and Maria certainly meant it when she refused him. But I love you, he would protest. But I don't love you, she would reply. Never mind, he would say, love's not important, it's respect that matters. But I don't respect you, she would say. Respect's not the be all and end all, he would say, just as long as we feel comfortable together. But I don't feel comfortable with you, she would say. Maria always stuck to her guns, credit where credit's due. And indeed she was only telling the truth, for she did not feel comfortable with Ronny, not comfortable at all, especially when he put his face very close to hers, and she could see the pimples and blackheads, and when he put his arm along the back of the seat upon which they were both sitting, and she could smell the sweat under his arms. And Ronny was not the worst, not by any means the worst.

In some respects, pretty salient ones by and large, she preferred Nigel to Ronny. For one thing he was not devoted to her. This meant that it was possible, sometimes, to have a sensible conversation with him. Maria considered conversation to be an overrated pastime, but occasionally she craved it, simply as a change from all the other overrated pastimes. It was Nigel's conversation which first impressed her. Ronny had chanced upon her one day in the street, and had insisted on taking her to a café for tea. They sat by the window, and were noticed by Nigel as he passed by the tea shop on his way back from a meeting of the Arbuthnot Society, a club for socialist chess enthusiasts. Maria was by no means attracted to him immediately, but she was nevertheless relieved that he came to join them, for Ronny had done nothing but stare moodily into her eyes for the last twenty minutes, and the tedium of the occasion was becoming staggering. He was clearly in no mood for talk himself, so Maria and Nigel began to talk to each other. In the course of their chat it emerged that both were labouring under a half-baked desire to see a new French film which was showing, for one night only, at a cinema in Walton Street. They agreed, therefore, to go together. Ronny was beside himself. He could not accompany them because, by a stroke of rank ill fortune, he was required that same night to attend, in his capacity as treasurer, a meeting of the Crompton Society, a club for existentialist bridge players. So he could only sit and watch, helpless, while his best friend, before his very eyes, arranged to go out with the girl whom he had loved for as long as he had known her.

Maria and Nigel spent a peculiar evening together. Before the film, they met for a drink, or at least met at a place where drinks were served, and drank there. We say, 'Shall we meet for a drink?', as though drinking were the main end of the appointment, and the matter of company only incidental, we are so shy about admitting our need for one another. When Nigel and Maria met for a drink, in other words, they were really meeting for a chat, to which the drink was no more than an oddly necessary accompaniment. After the drink, they went to the film, and after the film they went for another drink, or rather another chat because strange though this may seem after three hours together they did not yet want to part. And after the second drink, they went back to Nigel's room for coffee. Or at least, when they got back to Nigel's room, they drank coffee, but this was not the main purpose of their withdrawing there, because although I agree it surpasses belief, the fact is that after four hours they were still not tired of each other. We say, 'Would you like to come for some coffee?', as though it were less frightening to acknowledge that we are heavily dependent on mildly stimulating drinks, than to acknowledge that we are at all dependent on the companionship of other people. Funny, that. Several changes had already taken place in the nature of Maria's and Nigel's relationship by this stage, changes which, when Maria thought about it later that night, seemed hard to account for. For instance, when they emerged from the cinema, and walked from the cinema to the pub, they did so hand in hand. And when they emerged from the pub, and walked from the pub to the room, they had their arms around each other's waists. And when they emerged from the room, and said goodnight under a cloudless sky, they had their tongues in each other's mouths. Some people would call this progress. Maria didn't know what to make of it.

This was the start then of Maria's affair with Nigel. How significant, really, that the language affords no better word than 'affair' for this sorry procedure. How long it lasted, how much pleasure it gave them, these are details which we needn't bother with. However, a few words about the pastimes, the means of filling out the hours of empty fondness, enjoyed by this couple.

Before meeting Nigel, Maria had discovered only two ways of affording herself anything which she could honestly call enjoyment. They were listening to music, and being with Sarah. Now Nigel did not like music, and he did not like Sarah, so both of these had to go out of the window.

There were many things, on the other hand, which Nigel was not ashamed to admit that he enjoyed. Only three of them need concern us here, for in only three of them was Maria allowed to have any share.

One of Nigel's delights was to go to the pub and drink, with his friends, and now also with Maria. Many were the evenings on which he would take her to The King's Arms, or The White Horse, where she would like as not be the only woman among a circle of perhaps eight or nine men, all friends of Nigel's, all loud and jovial people, heavy and noisy and smoky and dark. The satisfaction derived by Maria from these entertainments was limited. It was not that Nigel's friends ignored her, although that would have been bad enough. Nor was it that their talk offended her, for Maria did not take offence easily, if ever. No, the sensation with which she would look back over such evenings was one of puzzlement. The friendship which bound these people together was not, she decided, of a sort which she could easily understand, and yet she tried. Of course she did not understand, for that matter, the friendship which had held her and Sarah together, but at least the comfort and the reassurance which they had found in that friendship had always been explicit, and it was its very explicitness, the delight they would take in expressing it, the delight each would take in witnessing the other's expression of it, which had made it all worthwhile, as far as Maria could see. For where was the comfort in all this boisterous aggression, what was the point of all this drinking, joking, thumping and laughing? This was what puzzled her. But if Nigel's friends puzzled her, then how much more, although they would never admit it, did Maria puzzle them. Are you all right, they would say. Cheer up, have another drink. It may not happen, they would joke. Maria always fell for this one. What may not happen, she invariably asked, and then the deafening roars, the yawning hilarity.

Sometimes, when Nigel did not want to take her to

the pub, he would take her to a party. Maria tagged along out of a sense of duty, or who knows, out of inclination, of a perverse sort. It would be stretching the truth, though, to suggest that she ever enjoyed the experience. Even she would admit as much to herself, sometimes. It would be hard to say which aspect of it she objected to most, there were so many. There was the heat, for example. Maria would wrap up warm, to go into the cold night, and then find, when she and Nigel arrived at the party, that the room was horribly hot, a consequence no doubt of the fact that it was crammed to the roof with people. And this also meant that Maria would find it difficult to move, or sit, or stand, without coming into closer contact with the other guests than she would have liked. And it meant, too, that the room would be extremely noisy, so that if Maria wanted to talk to one of the other guests, which, fair enough, she occasionally did, she would find it difficult to do so, so difficult, in fact, that she would be obliged to shout in order to communicate her ideas. Naturally, all the other guests would also be shouting, in order to communicate their ideas, or in some cases desires, so perhaps some exceptionally rational or level-headed person might have suggested, after calling a general silence by beating on the table with a stick, that everyone should henceforth talk, rather than shout, so that henceforth there would have been no further need for shouting. But such a person would have been misguided, for she, or he, would not have taken into account the fact that music was also playing, impossibly loud music, in order to encourage people to dance, or rather to shuffle, with as much freedom of movement as was consistent with a tolerable level of drink-spilling, and toe-treading, and knocking over onto the floor of bottles, and of people, with a crash. So not only did this make it doubly difficult for Maria to move, or sit, or stand, but it also made it doubly difficult for her to talk. And even when she did succeed in talking to one of the other guests, it was often, let's be honest, a let-down, because what possibility was there of interesting conversation, when all of the guests, to a man, and to a woman, were more than likely pissed out of their heads, almost as soon as and in some cases before the party began? Maria too would be pissed out of her head, she had no choice; but strange to say Maria pissed out of her head retained vestiges of rationality equal, one might say superior, to those which most of us attain even when sober. Drink seemed never to affect her reasonableness. And it is no fun, when you are in the mood for an interesting conversation, to receive nothing in response to your remarks except grunts, or yelps, or loud bellowing laughter or inarticulate expressions of sexual desire. For Maria often found herself to be the unwilling object of sexual desire, at times like this. Some-times she would wonder if she were the only person present whose immediate objective was not to achieve coitus with the nearest available partner, and at the earliest possible opportunity, which often as not meant there and then. And you would be wrong to think that Nigel was in any way a comfort to her in this situation, for he would not talk to her, or be with her, but would disappear early into the crowd and start making advances at whichever woman seized his wandering fancy. Which left Maria to stand and watch, apart but engulfed, removed but stifled, desperate, in her quiet way, for enjoyment, surrounded by what she had been encouraged to believe were its manifestations, and knowing nothing but this, that on none of the tired and wasted faces which thronged around her did she see the marks of real happiness, only the marks of a hateful delusion from which it seemed to be her privilege, and her burden, to be mysteriously free.

So much for parties. The third of his pleasures in which Nigel allowed Maria to share was sex. Indeed it might be argued that her co-operation, or at least participation, was in this instance essential, rather than accessory, to his enjoyment. But this is not quite true, for if there had been no Maria there would have been another woman, and even if there had been no other woman, Nigel could quite easily have satisfied his needs unaided, he had a pair of hands after all. It took him a week or two at first to entice Maria into his bed, and to gain admission to hers, but once the precedent had been established this interval decreased, until it could be done within a minute or two or in exceptional circumstances a matter of seconds. There is no need to give the details. Why describe all the gropings, the senseless fumbles and thrusts which this poor misguided couple executed upon each other on warm spring afternoons and clammy evenings? Why enumerate, in the hope of enlightening or perhaps even arousing the reader, the various gasps, kisses, groans, caresses, stains and clasps which characterize this ludicrous pantomime? Far better to forget, as Maria tried often and vainly to forget, the hours she had spent with this man in the flagging pursuit of a hazy gratification.

That then is the story of Maria and Nigel, the story of their love. Impossible to say how it ended, it faded away as all insubstantial things do. Sarah was waiting for her, of course, all this time, waiting to receive her when the moment came, which it did. And then all was well for a while. But the second year soon ended, and Maria and Sarah had to part, and not only for a few months, because Sarah's studies took her to Italy for the whole of the next year, Maria's last year. So that their days together, those days which had for both of them been nicer than most, were gone for good.

4. *The House*

The new academic year brought Maria a change of scene. One day during the previous term, her tutor had called her into her office.

'I have a proposition for you, Maria.'

Maria watched warily from her low armchair.

'When one has been at Oxford for as long as I have, teaching, working for the university, and when one is married to a man who has also taught, and worked for the university, for a long while, then one is bound to have accumulated a certain amount of – how shall I put it? – money. Now one doesn't want one's money to lie around idle, not doing anything, so one tends to invest it. My husband and I have chosen to invest our money in property. We own a small property, on the Iffley Road, which we rent out to students.'

A pause was left, in which Maria suspected that she was meant to manifest comprehension. This she did, by nodding.

'Naturally, we like to choose our tenants carefully. We like to take our pick of the students. My husband teaches at St John's, of course, but one of the first things we decided, was that we would prefer to let the rooms to girls, and to girls alone. And naturally, we look for certain

'. . . qualities, in a girl, before we make her an offer of rooms.'

'What qualities?' asked Maria eventually.

'We look, above all, for quietness of disposition. We look for girls who would benefit from being removed from the pell-mell of college life. We look for the withdrawing type.'

Maria, who was tired, very tired, of living in college, accepted her tutor's offer. Thus it was that she found herself living in Cribbage House, an establishment set up by the college authorities some four years previously as a means of farming out those students whose presence, for various reasons, they felt to be detrimental to the health of community life within college itself. It was a large house, comprising eight rooms, a shared kitchen, and two shared bathrooms. Structurally it was in need of repair. Most of the walls needed re-papering, or re-painting, or re-plastering, and most of the floors needed re-carpeting, except for those which had no carpets, which simply needed carpeting. There was rising damp, and dry rot, and woodworm. On the top floor, in the attic, colonies of fungi sprung forth from the walls. Downstairs, in the cellar, tribes of slugs and spiders flourished, sometimes making sorties to the upper floors in search of food, or perhaps just for the hell of it. The furniture was spare, to say the least, and fragile, to put it mildly. The whole house was supposed to be heated by a huge gas boiler which none of them knew how to operate.

Maria decided that it wasn't such a bad place.

She set about making her room more comfortable. First she bought herself a small electric fire, to go in the empty fireplace. It was on the mantelpiece above this fireplace that she arranged her books. Maria owned only one picture, a cheap framed print of Goeneutte's 'Boulevard de Clichy sous la neige', which she had bought some years ago, in a second-hand shop not far from St Jude's. She hung it on the wall opposite the fireplace. Her room was on the first floor, overlooking the road. There was a table, near the window, and a chair, near the door. She put the table near the door and the chair near the window. Once she had made these adjustments, she felt quite satisfied.

There was something about Maria's room which invariably led visitors, of whom there were very few, to remark, that although it was adequately, even ideally, suited to meet the basic contingencies of daily living, it was less than adequate, and much less than ideal, as a place in which to pass the night. This was that it contained no bed. Maria too had noticed this almost as soon as she had first entered it. There was a mattress on the floor, but nothing more. A thorough search led to the discovery of sheets and blankets in a cupboard in a disused room on the second floor. Maria complained to her landlady at once, and elicited the promise that a bed would be delivered as soon as possible. Two weeks passed, and still no bed arrived, but Maria did not renew her request because by now she had decided that she did not want a bed at all. In fact she was enjoying better rest than ever before. Rest rather than sleep, you notice. She would sleep for about half of the night and for the remainder she would lie awake, in the dark. But the word dark hardly does justice to the blackness to which Maria consigned herself when she turned off her light at midnight. This blackness, and this mattress, she believed, were the reasons why she always awoke feeling so rested. For the curtains, the dark blue curtains in Maria's room, were so thick, and so heavy, that not only was it hard work to close them, and to open them again in the morning, but also there was not a chance, not the slightest chance in a thousand, that a single ray of light from the sky or from the street outside should ever penetrate their soft defending wall. The dark in her room was absolute. Shadows and outlines didn't enter into it. It was relieved by one item only, and this was the tiny, unwinking red light emitted by her cassette player when connected to the power supply. Maria did not lie in the dark in silence, you see. She would have found that boring, and very probably have gone to sleep instead after only a few minutes. No, she listened to music, long into the night. Maria was particular about the music to which she listened in the dark. Once, a while ago, she had loved music, all music, any music, she used to devour it without discrimination, from records, from the radio, from concerts, even from her brother, in the days when he had been learning to play the violin, when she would sit with him in the evenings, in his bedroom, as he complainingly went through his exercises. Since then, she had grown increasingly careful, for she had started to notice that while some pieces of music seemed to purify her, and to clean her out, and generally to sharpen her perception, there were other pieces which contaminated, which cluttered her and clogged her mind with thick drowsy feeling. She had realized that music should be used sparingly, and never as an accompaniment, only ever as a focus of undivided attention. And it seemed to her that her attention could only ever be truly undivided when she lay quite still in the black. She would study her collection of tapes, choose one, insert it into the cassette player, depress the play button, and then quickly, as quickly as she could, turn out the light and lie on the mattress, pulling the bedding tightly around her, or, if it was a warm night, discarding it loosely until she was comfortable. By then the music would have begun. A few precious seconds wasted, that's all. And then for a while real joy, to hear and to understand this other language, to watch its beauty closely and to feel the guiding play of its proportions.

It would be tedious to mention all those works which Maria included in, and all those which she excluded from, her personal canon. A few examples. Most music after Bach sounded decadent to Maria, and decadence she abhorred. Bach himself could do no wrong. Her particular favourites were the suites for 'cello, and the sonatas and partitas for unaccompanied violin. Here the paths of melody could be followed without the distraction of any harmony other than that which was distantly implied. But anything by Bach always had the desired effect. She was fond too of the masses of Palestrina. What she hated most in music was inconsistency of dynamics. She could not tolerate the sudden change from pp to ff, and back again. By and large she disliked the piano, although there were pieces by Beethoven and Debussy which did not displease her. She preferred the chamber ensemble to the orchestra. She loved to be made sad by music, but this could only ever happen when she listened to music which pretended to no emotional effects. All that she ever asked was to be afforded a faint sense of wonder in the face of inaccessible beauty, a loveliness far in the future or far in the past, far off anyway, on which her attention would really be fixed while she stared, half-seeing, at the unwinking red light shining like a tiny beacon in the dark.

Cribbage House, although it contained eight rooms, had only four residents at this time. Thus four of its rooms stood empty, cold and locked. Maria had as little to do with the other girls as possible, although not out of ill-will. At first they all seemed nice enough to her (Maria was no judge of character, in the ordinary sense), but by now she was of the persuasion that people should have more to offer, if the fag of entering into human relationships were to be gone through, than mere nice-ness. And besides, as time passed, she began to have suspicions about these girls, she began to feel that their behaviour, not to put too fine a point on it, was odd, odd by any standards, not only the normal ones.

Their names were Anthea, Fanny and Winifred. Anthea was the most friendly, initially. She and Maria would sometimes walk into town together, to lectures, or to the shops, and sometimes go out together, to a film for instance, and even sometimes they sat in each other's rooms, talking, for company. Maria took a qualified satisfaction in all this. Then, one day, going into Anthea's room, when Anthea was out, in order to return a book, Maria noticed a notebook lying open on her desk. 'I hate Maria. I hate Maria. I hate Maria', it said, three times to a line, twenty lines to a page. There were forty-eight pages in the notebook and it was nearly full. Maria found this peculiar. And it was difficult, from then on, for her to talk to Anthea in quite the same way as before. They never spoke to each other again, in fact.

Fanny was neither talkative nor sociable, and Maria's feelings towards her were, for a while, entirely neutral. It was only after a few weeks that, putting various circumstances together in her mind, she began to entertain doubts. These circumstances were as follows. Certain small items belonging to Maria, those which tended, as it happened, to be worth the most, in material terms, had started to disappear from her room. Small items of jewellery, mainly, but also the occasional book and once a pair of shoes. Maria did not know whom to suspect of these little thefts, for thefts they surely were. One night, however, while she was using the bathroom, the thief came into her room and stole a small pendant. It was of no sentimental value, fortunately, it had been a present from Ronny. Maria saw that it was missing as soon as she returned to her room, and at the same moment heard

Fanny's door close on the other side of landing. Maria thought that this was curious, to say the least. A few days later, late at night, she was washing up, in the kitchen. She had taken her watch off and laid it on the table. After a few minutes Fanny came in, sat at the table wordlessly, and began to read the newspaper. Then, when Maria had finished her washing up, and came to retrieve her watch, she found that it was gone.

'Fanny,' she said, 'Give me my watch.'

Fanny looked up, feigning incomprehension.

'What?'

'My watch. You have stolen it. Please return it.'

'I don't understand.'

'You're a thief. You've been stealing my things for some time now. I know all about it.'

Fanny said nothing.

'Is it only me you steal from, or do you steal from the other girls as well?'

'No, only you,' said Fanny.

'Why?'

Fanny said nothing.

'Give me my watch back.'

Fanny produced Maria's watch, which she had secreted in her brassière, between her breasts. She stood up, and advanced towards Maria, who backed towards the sink. Fanny held out the watch. Maria took it, but as she did so, Fanny seized her wrist, and gripped it hard. Then she bent forward, and bit Maria on the shoulder. Maria cried out, and Fanny left the room without another word.

Maria found this behaviour surprising, although she was normally tolerant of other people's foibles, and following this incident, she and Fanny did not get on so well together.

'They seem like very nice girls,' Maria's mother said, one day in November when the family had all come to visit her. It was a dark Saturday afternoon and her mother, her father and Bobby were sitting around the electric fire. Tea had been served and drunk and there were a few biscuits left.

'I don't like them,' Maria said.

'Anthea is a striking creature,' said her father. 'A man could fall for her.'

'Why don't you like them, Maria?' her mother asked.

'We don't get on.'

'But Winifred has such a kind face. She was so kind to us while we were waiting here for you to come back. Is she not kind to you, Maria?'

Winifred was extremely kind to Maria, that was the problem. Maria tolerated her, however; she was undoubtedly the best of a bad bunch. But a short account must be given of this extraordinary girl.

Winifred was all that Maria wasn't, and more. She was an open, happy, confident and trusting person, who believed in the benevolence of God, the sanctity of marriage, and the innate goodness of human nature. She was moronic in other ways, too. For instance, she decided, on the basis of only a few days' acquaintance, not only that Maria was in need of help, but that she, Winifred, was the person to provide it. Accordingly she took pains to befriend her. And so she started to do small favours, she would perform little acts of kindness, such as to tap on Maria's door at seven o'clock in the morning with the words, Are you awake, Maria? A new day has dawned (as if this were anything to write home about) and I am just going downstairs to make you a nice cup of tea. This would perhaps not have been intolerable, were it not that Maria would have liked, occasionally, to have been allowed to sleep later than seven o'clock, and were it not that Winifred's methods of preparing tea were unorthodox, and consisted of placing a tea bag in a cup and then adding a mixture half of milk and half of water from the hot tap. Maria was tempted, naturally, to lock her bedroom door from the inside, but tended not to do so because on the one occasion when she had, Winifred had attempted to batter the door down with her shoulders and her bare hands, so determined was she not to deny her friend her early morning treat. You are too good, Maria, she had said. I know what you feel. You feel it is too much for me to take all this trouble over you every morning. Not at all. It is only by performing these little acts of kindness that I feel I can ever render myself useful to my fellow creatures. Open up at once. Maria had capitulated, then and subsequently.

Nor was this the only way in which Maria would find her privacy violated. Having drunk the tea (disposing of it by any other means was impossible, because Winifred would stay in her room and watch her until she had finished it) she would often find herself being summoned downstairs to the kitchen and served with a bowl of steaming hot porridge. This porridge took the form of great grey globules of muck. She might have used it to plaster over the cracks in the ceiling but that was about all it was good for.

'I wish you wouldn't do this for me every morning, Winifred,' she would say.

'Nonsense, dear, nonsense. If one can't light up the world with a few little acts of kindness now and again, then what is one worth, to be honest.'

Sometimes Maria would come in from the shops, a small bag of provisions in her hand, the materials from which to fashion a hurried meal as soon as the kitchen became vacant, and would find that Winifred already had a meal waiting for her, she would have cooked it herself, and she would not listen to Maria's protestations, she would be unmoved by her arguments, such as that the food which she had only just purchased would now be wasted. Instead, Winifred would stand over her and force her to consume of a heap of indigestible disjecta, a sun-beaming smile on her oval face the while, radiating from within a scorching consciousness of her own goodness.

'Did you like it, Maria?' she would ask at the end.

'Not really,' Maria would say, like as not scraping or prising half of it into the overflowing pedal bin. She would say it out of honesty, not out of malice, for she knew that no amount of malice could ever divert Winifred from her philanthropic path.

'Never mind, it was good and nourishing, and tomorrow I shall cook you something more tasty. What would you like?'

'I should like you not to cook for me.'

'Dear Maria.' Winifred took Maria's hand, and held it gently between hers. Maria attempted to recoil, but suddenly found that her hand was being held with a strength which it would not be inappropriate to compare to that of a vice. 'You are so good, and generous. It pains you, doesn't it, to see me put myself to any trouble on your account? But I don't mind, honestly I don't. It's a pleasure. Performing these little acts of kindness for you is the only real pleasure I have in the world.'

Hardly surprising, then, that Maria was not able to match her mother's enthusiasm. She did not dislike Winifred. She was baffled rather than frightened by her. All the same, her favourite time of day came to be the evening, when Winifred would not be around, for she usually went out in the evenings, to the meetings of charitable societies, and religious organizations. Often she would return from these meetings in a state of uncontrollable zealous excitement, and would find Maria and tell her all about it, sometimes if necessary rousing her from a deep sleep or interrupting her appreciation of a favourite piece of music. And if Maria were to lock the door again, she would simply hammer upon it until it was opened, or until the other two girls came to see what was the matter and the commotion became so great that Maria was no longer capable of ignoring it.

When Bobby asked Maria if he could stay with her for a night or two, therefore, she felt obliged to warn him about Winifred. She warned him that his sleep would probably be disturbed. But this warning turned out to have been unnecessary, and while Bobby was staying with her, Winifred said nothing to Maria, never once spoke to her or attempted to enter her room.

Bobby was now eighteen. He had left school, and was looking for a job. He had been unemployed for only a few months but already he was prone to fits of depression which lasted for anything up to a week, and his parents seemed to think that a short holiday with Maria in Oxford would do him good. This had been the purpose of their visit, to deposit Bobby. When the last of the biscuits had been eaten, and their parents had driven away, brother and sister were left, alone together in Maria's room. Bear in mind that these two had hardly spoken to each other for more than five years.

'It's nice to see you again, Bobby,' said Maria, after a long, but, it seemed to her, companionable silence.

'Do you get lonely here, on your own?'

'Yes, I do. Do you like it, living at home?'

'No, I don't. I want to leave. I'm glad I was able to come down here.'

'You're always welcome. You'll always be welcome, with me, wherever I am. You look very well.'

'Do I?'

'Yes. Do I look well?'

'No, Maria,' said her brother. 'You look older. And tireder. Do I really look well?'

'No,' said Maria. 'You look sad, and worried.'

'Perhaps things will turn out all right.'

They both smiled.

'Is Sefton well?' asked Maria.

'He's fine. I was talking to him only the other day. He was in fine spirits. We were in the sitting room, and I was asking him a few questions. I said to him, What's it all about, then? What do you think I should do? How do you view the career opportunities open to a man like myself, as an outsider, so to speak? As an impartial observer. You don't let these things get you down, I can see that, I said. Come on, what's the secret?'

'And what did he say?'

'He sort of stretched out on my lap, and purred, and took hold of my arm, and moved his claws in and out. It was very reassuring. I took it that he was advocating detachment. Indifference, even. Be idle, like me, that seemed to be the gist, there's no stigma really. Live life as it was meant to be lived. Half asleep, preferably. That was good enough for me. I dropped the subject. He seemed to be fishing for a short stroke, so I obliged, and then we dozed off together.'

'Does he remember me?'

'Oh, definitely. He's very fond of you.'

'I miss him.'

Strangely, they continued to talk for many more hours,

until ten o'clock, in fact. Bobby then realized that he had had nothing to eat.

'Is there a chip shop near here?' he asked.

Maria gave him the necessary directions.

'Aren't you coming?'

'No. I'm not hungry.'

'You look tired. Why don't you go to bed?'

'I might.'

Bobby borrowed his sister's front door key, and left. Maria, meanwhile, decided to take advantage of his absence by listening to some music. It might be her only chance to enjoy the blackness and the solitude. You should not assume from this that she resented Bobby's visit. On the contrary, as she made her preparations for bed that night, washing, undressing, choosing the tape, she did so in the consciousness of an unaccustomed warmth, a wholly unexpected rediscovering of kinship. But she was still reluctant to relinquish her midnight treat, the enjoyment of which had become increasingly import-ant to her, now that her relations with Anthea and Fanny had deteriorated, and now that the attentions of Winifred had intensified her need to feel capable of self-reliance. When she listened to Bach, alone, and saw nothing, these people ceased to exist. She suspected that Bobby would not understand this process, and besides, it would not work if there were somebody else in the room. So she listened, for about half an hour, to the first and second violin partitas, and then she fell asleep.

She was awoken by the sound of her bedroom door opening, and by light from the landing. It was Bobby.

'Hello,' he whispered.

'Hello,' said Maria. 'I must have fallen asleep.'

Sleepily she looked at her clock. It was four-thirty.

The next morning, as Bobby was toasting bread at the electric fire, Maria said:

'I had a very strange dream last night. I dreamt I was asleep, and then you woke me up by coming in, and I looked at my clock, and it was half past four.'

Bobby chuckled.

'What are you laughing at?'

'What happened after that?'

'I can't remember,' said Maria. 'What time *did* you come in last night? I never heard you.'

Bobby laughed again.

'That was no dream.'

'Oh Bobby, don't tease me. You can't possibly have been out that late. What time was it? I must have gone to sleep very quickly.'

'I was out,' said Bobby, 'until twenty past four. Your clock is ten minutes fast.'

Maria was both confused and alarmed.

'But where were you? What happened? What was wrong?'

Bobby laughed again, quietly and at length.

'One day, Maria,' he said, 'I shall tell you where I went last night. One day.'

'Never mind one day. Tell me now,' said Maria angrily.

Bobby shook his head, and kept his secret, for the time being. He stayed for two more days, cold, happy days. It was a windy afternoon when Maria said goodbye to him at the station. The sun kept making abortive efforts to penetrate dense banks of fast-moving cloud. The train was late, they stood chatting and holding hands, it grew warmer and less windy, and still Bobby would not explain. As his waving hand dwindled, Maria felt a sudden surge of loneliness. And then the sun really came out.

5. *Last Days*

Of all the Oxford days which Maria ever looked back on, she remembered none so clearly or with so much pain as a blazing summer's day at the end of her last term. It was a wasted day, an unhappy day, a very beautiful day in some respects. It started, as far as Maria's memory and therefore as far as we are concerned, in the afternoon. Armed only with a copy of poems by Baudelaire, which she had no intention of reading, she stationed herself on a bench, beneath a tree, opposite the main entrance to one of the men's colleges. It was astonishingly hot, and had been for about a week, the heat was beginning to have that weighty feel which means that a storm is not far off. It weighed her down, supplemented internally by the heat of anxiety and of desire. Her heart pounded, as hearts do at such moments, and in such situations, not an unpleasant feeling as long as it doesn't happen too often, more than once every few weeks, for example. In this position, which she varied only in a small way as we shall see, she waited for five hours, during which time she reflected haphazardly on the circumstances, the feelings and former incidents, which had brought her to this pretty pass. She did not recall them in chronological order, she did not so much recall them at all; in fact, it would be truer to say that they assaulted her, but we shall record them chronologically, for the reader's benefit.

She had first met Stephen shortly after waving goodbye to her brother at Oxford station, all those months ago. Maria was short of friends at the time. Her tutorial partner, a girl called Madeline, had noticed this and, being a horse of a different colour from those which inhabited Cribbage House, she had taken pity, what's more in quite a useful way. She had recognized immediately that there could be no real sympathy between Maria and herself, and so, rather than making an extravagant show of friendship, she had simply taken the trouble, over a number of weeks, to introduce Maria to most of her friends in the hope that some of them would like her, and that she, in turn, would like some of them. And indeed both of these hopes were, to a modest extent, realized, so that Maria needed no longer to be short of company on those days when she ventured into the city. She never took full advantage of this fact, it is true. For instance, she would never have called on one of these friends uninvited. But if she were to meet one of them by chance she would by no means hasten away, she would linger and talk, perhaps for a long time.

Of these new friends Maria had a particular favourite, whose name was Stephen. After waving goodbye to Bobby she had hurried off to her afternoon tutorial, and after her afternoon tutorial she had been invited back to Madeline's room, for a light tea, and also, did she but know it, for the opportunity to meet Stephen. Maria and Stephen had not got on, initially. She had thought him furtive, and he had thought her unfriendly, although both were wrong. In Maria's experience, boys either disliked her at once, or liked her at once, and if they liked her they would convert this liking, not knowing what else to do with it, into moonstruck love, droopy hangdog moody wide-eyed romantic slobbering, and if this emotion was not immediately reciprocated, which understandably enough it never was, they would adopt the absurd posture of the injured suitor, absurd enough in itself but fifty times more so if adopted within minutes of clapping eyes on the admired object. Now Stephen was very reticent with her at first, and so Maria assumed that this reticence had its origins in this same process, why after all should he be any different, and consequently she designated it with the word furtive, whereas in fact his only feelings towards her had been confusion, and an incipient liking which he had not known how to act upon. But Maria shortly came to realize her mistake. Meanwhile he had mistaken her distrust, her weariness, her abstraction and strange inner awareness of both loss and gain after the last two days with Bobby, all for unfriendliness. An inauspicious start, wouldn't you say. And yet out of this misunderstanding had grown a bond, and, on Maria's part at least, out of this bond had grown the stirrings of an attraction and an admiration so strong that they soon came to dominate her life and to seem, basically, a bit of a nuisance. At the same time she felt very happy, happier than she had done for months or even years, and it was a timeless happiness, too, free from the complications described in Chapter Three. It was qualified by one factor only, which was that she was not at all certain, she had no concrete evidence whatsoever, that Stephen returned her love. (And just when I was thinking that we could get away without using the word.)

Maria's love for Stephen (in for a penny) bore little relation to her love for Nigel. They never went to bed together. They never kissed. These were not Maria's decisions, she would have done both, simultaneously for preference. But at the same time she felt that it made a nice change not to do these things, it gave her a sense of independence to think that she could love without seeking routine satisfactions. Stephen himself never mentioned the matter. Occasionally Maria wondered whether he found her unattractive, or whether he was homosexual, or frigid, but more often she was happy to let things continue as they were. She had never had any use for wiles, the little feminine wiles in which it was considered by some indispensable to be adept. Charlotte, for instance, had found her attitude in this respect particularly hard to understand. You will never get anywhere, Maria, she had said once, until you learn to practise the ways, the little feminine wiles and ways by which we of the weaker sex are able to exercise our authority. Little gestures, Maria, and little actions, which render men helpless, which turn them to putty in our hands. These had turned out to be, in ascending order of effectiveness, the fluttering of the eyelashes, the crossing of the legs, and the sucking of

70

the penis. Maria was not impressed by this advice and had never acted upon it. She felt that it would be wrong, apart from anything else, to force upon Stephen attentions and pressures which he had not invited. She was happy already, and did not want to jeopardize her happiness.

Although I have, in this context, used the word happy (three times, not counting various derivatives), I have not, as you may have noticed, used the word content, and there is a good reason for this, namely that it denotes, does it not, a placid state of mind, and according to this definition Maria was not at all content, and was well aware of the fact, in lucid moments anyway. She was content to be in love with Stephen, she was content not to go to bed with him, but she was not by any means content not to know whether he was in love with her. Indeed torment would be a more useful concept to invoke than content, when describing the state of mind or, for that matter, of heart, into which this uncertainty had thrown Maria. Simply to know, as a matter of incontestable truth, that he did not love her, would have been much better than not to have a clue one way or the other. Her uncertainty led her into every manner of peculiar behaviour, for, in the absence of any definite information to the contrary, one half of her believed Stephen to be in love with her, and acted accordingly, whereas the other half held her back, and would not let her carry through to their conclusion actions which half of her patently craved. On such occasions her behaviour was, therefore, essentially that of a madwoman. And this afternoon, the one I am about to describe, was itself one such occasion.

There had been others, many others. Days when she had waited outside Stephen's college, knowing what time he was most likely to emerge in order to meet an appointment or an engagement, and had then followed him through the street, debating always within herself whether to approach him and to feign surprise, as if they had met by chance. Sometimes Maria could be very foolish. She knew that if Stephen ever found out about this behaviour, he would consider it incomprehensible, and might stop loving her, or might never start loving her, or might even stop liking her. Yes, might even stop liking her. But that didn't stop her doing it. There was one time which kept coming back to her, as she sat waiting outside his college that hot afternoon, it came back to her in fragments, glimpses insistent in form and character, always the same, but this is not how I shall narrate it.

It had been another warm afternoon, uncomfortably warm, but worth it for the lovely cool into which she had stepped as soon as she entered the chapel. She walked softly, her shoes echoing on the slabs, and sat unnoticed at the end of a pew, two rows from the back. The chapel was empty, except for the organ loft, where Stephen and his music teacher were having a lesson. Maria knew that Stephen had an organ lesson at this time in the afternoon, and had come to the chapel for this very reason, to listen to him as he played. It was the first time she had ever done so, and also the last, the memory being, as far as she could see, more important than the experience. It, the memory, came to take on a peculiar texture, composed largely in the end of visual rather than aural elements. Even now she felt a shudder, perhaps of pleasure, perhaps of pain, at the thought of the scene as her mind's and her remembrance's eye had between them framed it, the pale glowing tetragon of sunlight on the slabs, the shaft of sunlight connecting this figure to her nearest window, the dustclouds dancing before her, the shade around, and the soft, insistent music, to which Maria hardly listened, at least in her usual way, but which might have spoken to her of regretful acceptance, if she had been interested in that sort of conjecture. Now: irony coming up. The music, as far as Maria was concerned, was Stephen's. It was he who made it, and filled the chapel with it, it was he alone who was humanly responsible for the sound of those moments, for the sound which her world made, in other words, during that time. This was how she liked to look at it, and this was at the heart of all that day's worth. But to tell the truth, never a bad thing to do occasionally even in a novel, it had not been Stephen playing the organ at all, in this instance, for his teacher, exasperated beyond measure by the hopelessness of his performance, had taken over and played the whole prelude without stopping, as a demonstration of how it should be done. Maria did not know this. But her inaccurate memory meant much more to her than our knowledge of the facts can ever mean to us, so we needn't feel superior.

Since it was now approaching the end of their time at Oxford, things were getting desperate, from Ronny's point of view. None of his proposals of marriage had yet obtained a favourable response, in spite of the fact that he had increased their delivery to the rate of one a day. He had, of course, found out about Stephen. Ever since making the discovery, about six weeks ago, he had been the victim of an insane jealousy. What Maria never knew, when she followed Stephen through the streets of Oxford, the two halves of herself frantically debating whether or not to approach him, was that Ronny, more often than not, would be following her, frantically debating within himself (one cannot talk in terms of halves with regard to Ronny, eighths would be nearer the mark) whether to accost Maria, and charge her with her infidelity, or whether to accost Stephen, and confront him with his treachery, or whether to leave well alone. No decision was every arrived at, because he always lost them sooner or later. Ronny would have made a useless spy. But he knew all about their movements, he was well acquainted with the strange fascination which this quiet young man exerted, oblivious, over Maria. That was why, as Maria sat beneath the spreading tree, watching the entrance to Stephen's college, Ronny sat at the window of a nearby café, watching Maria through a pair of stolen opera glasses. He never once moved, except to order more cups of tea, his consumption of which soon ran into dozens, and to go to the lavatory, which he had to do more than he would have liked. At all other moments, his eyes were fixed on his prey. He sat sideways on his chair, poised to leap up should she make the slightest movement. He had no other idea than to follow her wherever she went.

This gave Ronny the edge over Maria, with respect to ideas. For she had not yet decided, had not really considered, for that matter, what she would do if and when Stephen emerged into the sunlight. We can only conclude, in fact, that she had not given either the motives or the consequences of her behaviour the slightest thought. Otherwise, how can we account for its absurdity? An absurdity apparent to everyone but Maria, apparent even to the passers-by who stared and shook their heads at the spectacle of her yearning vigilance. The best we can do is to surmise. Her course of action would probably have been to have hidden behind the tree, until he passed, and then to have called out, in an accent of surprise, Oh, hello, Stephen. And what she would have done after that is anybody's guess, for it would have depended entirely upon his response, and what his response would have been is nobody's business. I have enough difficulty predicting Maria's behaviour, without bothering about his. From this quagmire of speculation, however, one fact can be retrieved. This is that it was essential, for Maria, that the encounter should seem to be unplanned. Explain that if you can. Perhaps she thought that Stephen might be disposed to interpret a chance meeting as the sign of fate's intervention, and would thereby conclude that he and Maria were made for one another, or something like that. Or perhaps she wanted to be in command of the situation, and felt that the odds were better if it were only she who knew the circumstances by which it had come about. Perhaps (getting warmer) she did not want him to know how desperately she had wanted to see him again. Perhaps, therefore, we can explain the whole daft phenomenon by reference to a certain vice, five letters, beginning with p and ending with e, not entirely unconnected with a certain unfortunate incident which took place in a certain garden, shortly after the dawn of time, if you can remember that far back. There is obviously a very wholesome lesson to be drawn from this. Maria might have spared herself a great deal of unhappiness, it's hard to say exactly how much, no more than a lifetime's worth at the most. Anyway, guesswork can only go so far.

Part of Maria's foolishness can be traced to the fact that her relationship with Stephen had recently drawn to a climax of aching ambiguity. It was the end of term and he was going away the next day, not home, but away, far away, to China, in fact, where he was to take up a teaching job. He would have gone earlier, but he had to stay in Oxford for a viva, that very afternoon, Maria didn't know when exactly, which is why she was waiting outside his college all afternoon, for she knew that his route lay that way. The previous evening, alone together, in a bar, they had talked about his journey, he with a mixture of apprehension and excitement, she with a mixture of anguish and misery, neither of which he noticed, in his apprehension and excitement. Oh, but they had come so close, so very close, to a declaration of shared feelings. There had been moments when their hands had nearly touched, and their eyes had nearly met, and after that it might all have been plain sailing, love offered and reciprocated, nothing new really but it seems to mean a lot to the people involved. It never quite happened. I shall miss you, Stephen, she had said. I shall miss you, Maria, he had said, with emphasis on the 'you'. Would you like me to come with you? Maria never said this, although she wanted to say it, she was dying to say it. I would like you to come with me. He had never said that either, although perhaps he too wanted to say it, but didn't, out of shyness. Well, I suppose this is it. That's what he did say, as they stood out in the dark after closing time and said goodbye. Maria now came close, very close, to asking her question, but all she had managed was to falter, If there's anything you want, before you go. Yes, he had asked, when she tailed off. You know my number, she said. You know my number.

She had not slept that night, or listened to music.

Maria waited for five hours outside Stephen's college. After one and a half hours, he had left for his viva by a back route, known only to members, and after another hour he had returned, the same way. He had then spent three hours packing, and had left for the station, by the front route, but by then Maria herself had left, in despair, and slightly pissed off with the whole business. And Maria chose to get up and leave, as it happened, at a time when Ronny was in the lavatory, so he neither saw her go nor knew where she went. The afternoon had not worked out too well all round.

It was a clammy summer evening. Maria wandered carelessly. She tried to hear Stephen's music again, in her mind, she played it back as an accompaniment to the fading busy life all around her. She sobbed, who wouldn't, but most of all she chided herself for the waste, the senseless anxiety she had inflicted that afternoon. All the long evening she lay by the river, tired, angry, waiting for the light to die once and for all. Then she walked home (for want of a better word. And, indeed, for want of a better place).

On arriving at Cribbage House, she was met by the sight of Fanny slowly and silently carving grooves in the kitchen table with the bread knife. Maria looked in, withdrew, crossed the dark hallway and began to climb the stairs. But she was stopped by a voice, Fanny's voice, Fanny who had not spoken to her since their fight over the watch.

'Maria.'

Maria halted, turned.

'Yes?'

'A man rang.'

Maria came down one step.

'When?'

'I can't remember.'

'Did he give his name?'

'No.'

'Did he leave a message?'

'No.'

She watched her face for signs of malevolence, and saw

none. Not wishing to cry in front of Fanny, Maria ascended the stairs quickly. Her bedroom door slammed.

*

She was awoken at about three in the morning by the sound of thunder. The storm had broken. Sleepily she listened to the rain battering her window, and the periodic crashes, forgetful in her drowse of the unhappiness which had so recently descended on her. No glimpse of the lightning was admitted by the thick, dark blue curtains, but soon Maria, impatient of this deprivation, got up from her mattress and threw them open. Then she sat by the window and watched the rivers of rain coursing down the glass, and the huge blue garish streaks splitting the sky. Sitting there, strangely frightened and fascinated, she must finally have fallen asleep again, because she felt a sudden jerk of consciousness and an instinctive sense of time lapsed when she first heard the sound of familiar feminine fists banging on her door. She swore silently but went to admit Winifred at once, knowing well that resistance was futile.

She had expected to see a smiling face, to be subjected to a shrill torrent of praise for the splendour of the storm and the proof which it afforded of God's majesty. But Winifred was very quiet, very solemn as she entered the room, wordless, and stood gravely by the fireplace, her head bowed. She was also very wet, and cold. Maria fetched a blanket from a drawer, and draped it around her shoulders, but she seemed hardly to notice.

'Maria – ' she began at last, and then stopped.

'Is anything the matter?'

'Yes,' she faltered. 'At least I think there is. Maria, you must advise me, you must tell me what you think. I think – I think I may have done a bad thing.'

'Can't you remember? Aren't you sure?'

'I know I did it. I know that. But I want you to tell me, whether you think I did the right thing, or the wrong thing.'

There was a pause for thunder.

'Well, you'd better tell me what it is.'

'There was this man, you see. A young man, I should think just a little bit older than us. He came up to me in the street, and – well, I killed him.'

Maria was for some reason speechless.

'Well, what do you think? Is that a bad thing . . . to have done?'

'Winifred, are you sure you did this? You're not just making it up? When did it happen?'

'Just now. I came straight back here. It happened in town.'

'Tell me,' Maria sat down on the mattress, the strength having left her body, 'tell me more about it.'

'Well,' Winifred took a breath, and then went on, in a shaking voice, 'as you know, I'd been to the usual meeting, the Holy Truth Society, the one I go to every week, and we'd had the usual talk, this week it was about yoghurt, and after the talk we'd had a good discussion. Really,' she reflected, 'a very good discussion, and after this discussion we went back to Marjorie Ogilvie's rooms, as usual – this would be at about half past ten – and she gave us some things to drink and of course some drugs – just mild hallucinogenics, you understand, it's a little weakness we indulge occasionally – and after that, well, it all begins to get a bit hazy. I can remember us all arguing about Aquinas's theory of the angelic hierarchy – there must have been only five or six of us there by now, as well as this big blue rabbit in the corner who seemed to be taking an unnecessarily anti-Thomistic line – and then all I can suppose is that I fell asleep, because the next thing I knew it was three o'clock in the morning and I had this funny sensation, it was as if my tongue was two hundred feet long and all coiled around the lampstand, I don't know if you've ever had it. Anyway, Marjorie seemed to be turning us all out, so I managed to get downstairs and outside and I found myself in the middle of the storm. I was starting to feel very cold, and sick, and to think a bit more clearly, and I walked along for a while until suddenly I realized that I was completely lost. That was when this man came up. This beastly man. I was sheltering from the rain in this doorway, when he came up with his umbrella and offered to take me home. Where do you live, he said. I knew this was in the nature of a proposition, I could tell he was . . . propositioning me. You piece of filth, I said, you lump of scum, leave me alone. Hush, he said, hush, you're lost and I want to take you home. Let me help you, he said. So I shouted, Leave me alone with your depraved filthy cravings, let me be. I know what you want, it's my body you're after. And then, and then, do you know what he said? I wouldn't say no, he said, I wouldn't say no to a bit of your body at all. So then I – then I think I must have snatched his umbrella off him and started poking him in the face with it, and when he fell over I can remember shutting it and hitting him over the head with the handle, it had this heavy wooden handle, and then . . . and then I came back here.'

There was a long silence. Except, of course, for the storm.

'Where is the umbrella?' Maria asked.

'It's in my bedroom.'

'And you're sure he was dead when you left him?'

'Oh yes,' said Winifred, half smiling with satisfaction in spite of herself. 'I made quite sure of that.'

Maria got up, and forced herself to lay her hand gently on Winifred's shoulder.

'I think you should go to bed,' she said. 'Go to bed, and have a nice long sleep. And then, when you wake up, you might find that it was all a horrible dream.'

'Do you think so?' said Winifred.

'Yes, I do.'

'Do you know what, Maria,' said Winifred, after a few moments' pause, 'that's good advice. I think that a rest is exactly what I need. Everything will seem much clearer in the morning.'

When Winifred, this resolve notwithstanding, failed to

move, Maria took her by the arm and led her back to her bedroom. Then she went back to bed. The storm was on the wane and, rather to her own surprise, she fell into a deep and restful sleep.

The next morning, as she was getting dressed, Maria heard a car draw up in the drive outside Cribbage House. Doors slammed, and there was an impatient ring on the doorbell followed eventually by the sound of two men climbing the stairs. She heard them knocking on Winifred's door and then questioning her in quiet hostile voices. Maria looked out of the window and saw, as she had expected, the shiny blue roof of a police car. She decided to leave as quickly as possible. Furtively, Maria slipped on the remainder of her clothes, opened her door and slid through the doorway, tiptoed across the landing, stole down the stairs and sidled towards the front door. As soon as she was free she broke into a run, and continued in what was never less than a breathless stride until she had reached the town centre.

There she paused, uncertain. A curious desire now took shape within her, one which she had never felt before and which on any other day would have appalled her, namely, the desire to visit Ronny. Since we are duty-bound to attempt an explanation of this aberration, maybe the case was simply that his mindless adoration was at this stage the only dependable factor in her life, the only form of affection accessible to her when most in need of support. She felt oddly reassured by the thought of seeing his stupid smile, even of receiving the inevitable offer of marriage and of watching his face fall as she softly refused him. Pathetic behaviour, this, without a doubt, but she's been under a lot of strain.

Ronny's delight and surprise upon seeing her lie outside the emotional range of this book. Naturally he wanted to know what had brought about her change of heart.

'Well, I just thought . . . we both have so little time left in Oxford. I wanted to say goodbye properly.'

'Goodbye? But we'll see each other again. We'll still see a lot of each other, from now on.'

'We can't rely on that, Ronny. I don't even know what I'm going to do next, or where I'm going to go.'

'Wherever it is, I'll be there.'

Maria did not seem to take from this statement the reassurance which Ronny had intended.

'Don't be silly,' she said. And then, to change the subject, 'Look, it's nearly twelve o'clock. Why don't we go for a drink, and some lunch?'

They went to a pub in St Giles'. As they walked there, Ronny could not help observing that Maria seemed extremely depressed. He based this conclusion, with what counted for him as startling psychological insight, on various slight and subtle signals, such as her reluctance to raise her eyes even momentarily from the pavement, and her refusal to speak a word even in response to direct questioning. His usual way of injecting cheerfulness into a conversation with Maria was to make earnest promises of accompanying her for the rest of her life, and supporting her through the direst financial and emotional difficulties.

But today, this failed to have the desired effect. Fortunately their arrival at the pub presented his limited imagination with a new subject for discussion.

'What would you like to eat?' he asked.

'What are you having?'

'Well, the gammon's very good here. But perhaps you don't feel like hot food on a day like this. They do excellent salads.'

It took Maria a long time to make up her mind, since she had no appetite whatsoever and therefore no criteria on which to base her decision. But finally she chose the gammon.

Gammon. That was her first mistake.

6. *Her First Mistake*

Six years later, as the unfortunate consequence of having chosen to eat gammon on that hot afternoon, Maria is sitting in silence with her husband at the family breakfast table. Her son Edward, aged four, is contemplating with resentment the egg which his mother has once again failed to boil to his satisfaction. Maria's state of mind is one of misery, a misery such that I cannot describe and you probably can't imagine, so we'd better just leave it. Martin, her husband, is reading the newspaper, or at least pretending to, for in fact he is secretly preoccupied with a scheme which his next words will introduce, and of which Maria has not, as yet, the least inkling. It is summer again, warm indoors and out.

It is customary, of course, when it comes to stories like this, to believe whatever the author tells you, and yet I can imagine that for some of you there might be a problem in taking at face value my assertion in the first sentence of this chapter. I repeat, that if Maria had not chosen gammon, she would not have married Martin. For gammon, as you know, is often very salty, and liable to induce thirst, and if Maria had not been thirsty she would have had no reason, no reason whatsoever, to go into a tea shop that afternoon after saying goodbye to Ronny.

And if she had not gone into the tea shop, she would not have chanced upon her old friend Louise, and if she had not chanced upon Louise, Louise would not have invited her to a party that night. And she would not have gone to the party, and she would not have met Martin, for where else could she have met Martin, who lived in Essex and had never been to Oxford in his life before or since? She had never loved him, and he had never loved her, but he was looking for a wife and she was looking for something to do, so they seemed as well suited as most couples ever are. They had a whirlwind courtship, consisting of much sex and a bit of theatre-going, married in October, honeymooned on the Riviera, and produced their first and only child exactly sixteen months later. Maria was by now twenty-three, pushing twenty-four, and she was already aware that she had made a bad mistake.

Finally Martin laid down his newspaper and coughed. Maria sensed that he had something important to say. She stiffened imperceptibly in her chair.

'How long have we been married now, Maria?' he asked.

Edward forgot about his boiled egg and began to look on with interest.

'Five years,' she said, 'and nine months.'

'Hmm . . .' Martin leant back in his chair, and gazed at the ceiling as if in thought. 'In that case . . . in that case I think it's about time we got a divorce.'

Maria looked at Edward.

'Edward, why don't you run upstairs and play? Why not colour the book I bought you, and then I'll come up and see how well you've done.'

'I'd rather listen,' said Edward, whose delight it was to refuse everything his mother asked of him.

'The child can listen if he likes,' said Martin. It was a family trait.

'On what grounds?' asked Maria.

He pretended not to have understood her.

'On what grounds do you want a divorce?'

He made a show of deliberation.

'There are a variety of grounds, of course,' he said, 'on which I could divorce you. You have not been a good wife to me. You are not a good mother to little Ted.' Here he patted the child on the head. Edward smiled. 'There are various arguments, in short, which I could put forward to a court of law. For instance, you do not fulfil my sexual needs. For some time now you have made no effort to fulfil my sexual needs.'

Effort, indeed, was a desideratum when it came to fufilling Martin's sexual needs. Physical effort of a high order. Maria had not suspected this at first, she had thought him a gentle lover. They had lain in bed together, naked for obvious reasons, and he had touched her so lightly, drawn closer to her so gradually, that she had not been afraid of him at all. Love making had been a pleasure, unaccountable though this may seem. Anyway, that had not lasted for long, it stopped soon after the wedding in fact. Maria was surprised, therefore, to find after eight months that she was carrying a baby, for the forms of intercourse which Martin enjoyed, and in which she was his unhappy accomplice, were not such as would normally lead to conception. Violence came to play an important part. Nothing nasty, just the occasional stranglehold or bite, it was rare for him actually to kick her in the face at such moments. All the same he did beat her sometimes, it was difficult to know why and Maria always forgot to ask at the time. She had nobody to tell about it, because she and Martin now lived in Essex, where she had no friends except for a few neighbours, women mainly older than Maria who came round for coffee now and then in the morning, and tea in the afternoon, but who never ventured to inquire whether the weals on her neck were the marks of sexual passion or merely of anger; and even if they had, Maria may not have been able to remember. No, their conversation mainly concerned vegetable prices, and the respective merits of various brands of soap powder, and the advantages and disadvantages of wearing make-up. Not that Maria wasn't interested in these questions as well, for Martin let her have very little money to buy food (he never did any shopping himself) and insisted that the house be kept clean (although he never helped to clean it) and insisted that Maria should look nice (or what he considered to be nice). So these things were important to her, too. But there never seemed to be much sympathy between Maria and her neighbours, or fondness, or friendship, or even liking. In fact it was as much as she could do to put up with their company for more than half an hour at a time.

'Why do you want a divorce?' she asked now. 'Have I done something wrong?'

'No, I wouldn't say you've done anything wrong,' said Martin. 'But five years is long enough to be married to any woman, in my opinion. To tell you the truth, you have started to bore me. You have been boring the living daylights out of me for several months now.'

'I see.'

Maria could not meet her husband's eye. She looked to her son for support, but this was a complete waste of time. He had shifted his chair closer to his father's, and the two of them were holding hands under the table. She got up slowly and carefully, walked to the kitchen window, and stared out.

Why, though, had she herself not divorced Martin years ago, on the grounds of mental cruelty, on the grounds of physical cruelty, on any one of any number of tenable grounds? She had considered the idea, often enough, but had always decided against it, for the sake of her son, Edward. Perhaps this seems out of character. For instance, Maria has not, until now, appeared particularly self-sacrificing, and she has not, until now, appeared particularly stupid, and yet stupid she would surely have to be not to have noticed that Edward bore towards her the sort of malice which stood every chance of ending in matricide. Yes, of course Maria had noticed this, and yet she loved her child. She knew full well that he adored his father (they were kindred spirits, after all). She knew too that nothing would make Edward hate her more than to be taken away from him. At the same time she believed that to leave Edward to the care of his father alone would be to destroy him. She cherished a rather loopy conviction that if only she were to persist, to offer the ungrateful infant all that she could in the way of maternal affection and attention, she might yet save him from the path he was set upon, which seemed at present to be that of a psychopathic killer. Her motives here were not entirely selfless, all the same, for the desire to see her son improve his character was not quite as strong as her determination that she should one day win his love.

'What about Edward?' she asked, turning.

'I beg your pardon?' said Martin, with polite surprise.

'Who will keep Edward? Who will bring him up?'

'Why, I will, of course. Who did you think?'

'Sometimes,' said Maria, hardly knowing why she went on, 'it is customary for the mother to retain custody of her child.'

'I hardly think that is likely to happen in this case,' said Martin, 'although, if you think the matter is worth bringing up, perhaps we might at least consult the boy's own inclinations.' He turned to Edward and ruffled his dark hair gently. 'Well, Ted, who would you rather stay with, your mother or your father?'

'You, Daddy,' said Edward.

Maria, putting up a resistance which seemed more and

more irrational, said, 'No court would take his wishes into account. He's too young.'

'They would too,' said Edward.

'You don't know what you're doing?' Maria shouted.

'If they didn't listen to me, then I'd tell them.'

There was a short silence.

'Tell them what, Ted?' his father asked, in a very quiet voice.

'How she tried to kill herself.'

Maria gasped.

'How do you know that?'

'I told him, naturally,' said Martin. 'The boy has a right to know these things.'

So, for that matter, has the reader. I should tell you, then, that on at least two occasions following her marriage to Martin, Maria had attempted to take her own life. It was on the basis of this fact that I ventured earlier to describe her state of mind as one of misery, a word usually to be treated with caution but which seemed, after mature consideration, to fit the bill in this instance. For it is very hard, as a general rule, to judge people's states of mind from external circumstances, and yet it occurred even to Martin that his wife was, perhaps, slightly cheesed off when, returning home from work one evening, he caught her in the very act of trying to do herself in. For Heaven's sake, dear, he had said, take your head out of the oven and pour me a gin and tonic. He had had a hard day at the office. Exactly how he felt about Maria's suicide attempt is hard to determine, for it is very hard, as a general rule, to judge, etc., but my guess is that he was neither especially surprised nor displeased, since it increased after all his hold over her. All he had told her, anyway, was that it is no longer possible to kill yourself by putting your head into a gas oven. You can do yourself a mischief that way but this is hardly the same thing. Maria took careful notice of his advice and next time tried to do it by overdosing on sleeping pills. A messier business altogether, and one which, after four and a half hours cooling his heels in a hospital waiting room while his wife had her stomach pumped, he found it much harder to accept with equanimity. It was this incident which he had reported to his son, who received the information, as far as I know, with perfect composure, seeming to expect no less from his mother. Extraordinary sang froid for a three-year-old, I think you'll agree. Maria had made no further efforts to do away with herself. There had been days when she had contemplated it, but the last attempt had shaken her up rather, and she had no particular desire to put herself through indignities like that again.

There were only two people to whom she ever con-fessed her unhappiness (two people and one cat, to be precise, but her visits home were by no means frequent). Incredulity will no doubt rear its ugly head again when I tell you that the first of these was Ronny. Not that she saw Ronny very much, for he now lived in London, and there subsisted between him and Martin a hatred of such intensity that it would have been on the whole tactless for him ever to have come to visit them in Essex. He had been mortified to hear of the marriage, and when Maria, during the early months of her pregnancy, had first come to visit him at his London flat, he had initially refused to see her, and such was his pique that it took him more than three minutes to relent. Subsequently, however, he had invited them both to dinner, and it was on that evening, an evening disastrous for other reasons (Ronny was a hopeless cook) that he and Martin had first conceived their fierce and mutual detestation.

'I can't eat any more of this,' Martin had said, hurling his knife and fork into the fireplace. 'It's like trying to eat a plate of shit.'

'It doesn't surprise me in the least,' said Ronny, 'to learn that the sensation of eating excrement is familiar to you.'

Maria looked helplessly from one to the other.

'I like this wine,' she said brightly. 'Where did you get it?'

'If you ask me, he pissed into the bottle,' Martin quipped.

'Your inability to distinguish between urine and Sauvignon '75 surprises me, I must say,' answered Ronny. 'May I ask where you were brought up? In a barn, I presume.'

'At least I don't live in a bloody barn, that's more than can be said for some people. Where did you get this furniture, the local tip?'

'Darling, please don't be rude,' said Maria. 'Ronny will get upset.'

'I shall never be upset,' Ronny said, 'by the guttural

94

chatterings of a malignant baboon. When your charming husband utters a word of sense, then I shall respond accordingly.'

'Fuck face,' came Martin's riposte.

'Dick nose,' Ronny countered.

And yet the curious thing was, that Martin could be quite polite about Ronny in his absence. You have a letter from Ronny, I see, he would say at the breakfast table. Is he well? Read me out the interesting bits.

But Maria would never read any of it out loud, because Ronny's letters to her were usually along the following lines:

Dear Maria,

I hope you are well. I love you and want only to devote the rest of my life to your service. My only wish is to be near you, my only hope is to tear you away from the monster to whom you are wed and to lay myself at your feet. If ever you need me, my darling, I will be here, ready to follow your footsteps wherever they lead. Everyevening I sit by the telephone waiting for you to call.

Maria, divorce Martin and marry me. I worship you. I have always known that my only purpose in life is to bring you happiness. Be mine.

The car is at the garage again. The man says the plugs need changing.

Eternally yours,
Ronny.

Once, Maria would simply have given these letters a cursory reading, and then consigned them to the pedal bin along with the bacon rinds and discarded scraps of fried bread. But now she always folded them carefully, replaced them in their envelopes, carried them up to her bedroom and locked them away in a secret drawer. A secret drawer, I should add, the existence and function of which were perfectly well known to her husband, who had long ago supplied himself with a spare key, and whose habit it was, whenever Maria was in the bath, to while away many a pleasant half hour in reading, and chuckling, over Ronny's insane avowals of devotion. Thus it was, this morning, that he was able to say:

'Of course, I have plenty of evidence.'

'Evidence of what?' said Maria, by now lingering in the kitchen doorway, longing to run upstairs, the tears glistening against her pale skin.

'Evidence of your infidelity to me. Your adultery. Your obscene violation of our marriage contract.'

'I have never been unfaithful to you.'

At this moment Maria felt a peremptory hand on her shoulder, and she stepped aside to let a figure pass through the doorway into the kitchen. It was Angela, Edward's nanny, a woman some two years Maria's junior, whose services had been engaged during the long trip to Italy which Maria had made the previous year. Her presence absurdly gave Maria a new energy for argument. She believed that here she had a silent witness for the defence.

'Who do you mean? Who have I ever betrayed you with?'

'I'm talking, my dear, about your unchastity, your vile prostitution with your lover Ronald. Your old tumescent schoolfriend. That putrid penis you knew at Oxford.'

Maria said quietly, 'Ronny and I are friends. We have never made love.'

Martin laughed.

'Of course, I don't believe that, and neither would a court of law. But in any case it's quite beside the point. The point is that I have written documentation of your affair. Dozens, scores, hundreds of letters written to you in a ferment of passion. I have taken xeroxed copies of these letters and placed them in the vault of the bank. I have had them scrutinized by a team of highly qualified handwriting specialists. I have had your friend shadowed by a crack squad of private investigators. I know that he frequently spends all his spare time writing to you. I have had his telephone tapped, and have recordings of compromising conversations conducted by the pair of you for fifteen minutes at a stretch. Conversations in which you told him the most palpable lies about my treatment of you. Lies which can be refuted by a trustworthy and disinterested witness. Angela, darling . . .'

Both Maria, who had been leaning against the door-post, facing the hall, and Angela, who had been wiping the draining board, turned sharply when they heard these words. Angela in response to the summons, and Maria because she was shocked to hear the nanny addressed with a term, and in a tone, of endearment. Within seconds a sudden and inevitable suspicion had formed, grown, and withered into knowledge.

In order to account for her original decision to employ a nanny in the household, it is necessary to identify the second person in whom Maria had been wont to confide the true state of her marriage. This was none other than her old and dear friend, Sarah. Sarah had returned from Italy a few months later than expected, and had been back at Oxford for more than a term before she got around to locating her old companion. Maria was pregnant by now, and passably cheerful. Sarah was pleased to find that she was married, following the doubts which she had once expressed about Maria's suitability for that state in a conversation which had made a deep impression on the minds of both women, and which I have helpfully recorded in Chapter Three. Are you happy, Maria, she had asked, just to make sure. This was a word, as you know, towards which Maria's feelings were ambivalent. I suppose so, she had answered.

Maria may not have known what happiness was, but she could recognize unhappiness when she saw it, and she was seeing plenty of it by the time that Sarah next contacted her. This was not for a while. Sarah had by now left Oxford. Are you happy, Maria, she had asked again, just for form's sake. I suppose so, Maria had answered, but her answer in this case was promptly invalidated when she immediately burst into tears and sobbed on Sarah's shoulder for no less than thirty-five minutes. (You will have noticed that Maria has started to develop quite a tendency to give vent to her emotion in this way. Don't worry, it won't last.) She did not go into details, however, on this occasion. It was not until another year had passed, or more, I get so confused about time, that she let everything out, all the secrets of her terrible mistake. She told Sarah the lot, she even showed her the marks. Sarah was speechless, she had nothing to say, in fact her first response was to burst into tears and to sob on Maria's shoulder for no less than thirty-five minutes. Divorce him, was her eventual advice. But Maria would not, for the frankly feeble reasons given earlier. Time and again, then and subsequently, Sarah attempted to persuade her to leave her husband. But the child, Maria would say, and besides, where would I go, and what would I do. Finally Sarah was able to answer this question. She was offered a temporary job at a school in Florence, and her employers rented a house for her, a great, crumbling palazzo on the north side of the city. It was far too big for her to live in alone, so she invited Maria to come and stay for as long as she could. But the child, said Maria. Nevertheless Sarah's invitation was so pressing that she summoned the courage to ask Martin whether he would approve the idea of her taking a long holiday, for the sake of their marriage, as she rather quaintly put it. To her surprise, Martin was agreeable, although in fact there was nothing very surprising about this at all, he was profoundly bored with Maria's company and the originally very limited fun of kicking her about the house was already wearing off. He suggested that a nanny should be engaged to look after Edward, and chose for this purpose Angela, a typist from his office with whom he had been having an athletic sexual relationship for several months. Maria did not suspect this, for some reason. But then she had gone very soft since her marriage.

And so for nine months she enjoyed freedom, a sort of freedom anyway, the freedom to live in one of the world's great cities, away from her husband. They were happy days, full and enriching, sunny for the most part but with always, in some corner or other, an element of shade, and not the cool and beckoning shade to which one retreats from the blaze, but the advancing gloom, dank and noisome, of her return to England and to Martin. Towards the end of her holiday this shade became so oppressive, so consuming, that Florence came for Maria to be a place of horror, and she decided to cut short her stay, leaving early one morning after writing a hurried note to Sarah, and arriving home the next day, nearly a month sooner than her husband had been expecting her.

'There's just one thing, Maria,' Martin had said, that evening, after they had eaten together, and talked, for all the world as if they were a happily married couple pleased to be together again after long separation, 'I think that Angela should continue to live here. You will find her a great help. Edward, of course, has become very attached to her. She has become indispensable to me.'

Maria now knew what he had meant.

'You called her darling,' she said.

Martin ignored this comment, or possibly didn't hear it, for it was spoken very quietly.

'You will confirm, won't you, my sweet,' he said to the nanny, sliding his arm around her waist, 'that I have been the tenderest and most considerate of husbands to Maria. You would tell the court, wouldn't you, love of my life, of her ill treatment of Edward, her cruel neglect, her failure to fulfil her obligations towards her loyal and devoted spouse.' He turned to Maria. 'Angela and I will marry, of course. I spoke to the vicar about it last night. The honeymoon is all arranged. We fancy a short cruise, in the Mediterranean. The tickets are all booked.'

'Supposing,' Maria began, but couldn't be bothered.

'There is no chance, my dear, simply no chance at all, of my losing the case. A divorce will be granted, on the grounds of irretrievable breakdown of marriage. Even if I choose, out of motives of sheer human decency, to suppress the fact of your adultery, I will have no difficulty in proving unreasonable behaviour. You failure to satisfy me sexually is evidence enough of that. Can you consider the humiliation involved, the self-hatred, in having to turn to a servant, a mere domestic dogsbody, for physical gratification? As for the custody of Edward, there will be no argument about that. Your unsuitability as a mother is obvious. You have attempted suicide. You have deserted him and left him to be brought up by a complete stranger while you cavorted around Europe. The court will have no hesitation in giving him over to the care of his father and his beloved nanny.'

After a silence, the nanny asked, 'Are you going to put up a fight?'

She looked at her husband, and shivered, and shook her head. Maria knew when she was beaten.

7. Redunzl

To lose her son pained Maria no end, but to be free of Martin was in every other way a relief. It freed her to move to London, and to live with Sarah, to enter, in fact, upon one of her better phases. This is going to make for rather boring reading, I'm afraid. Such periods are more interesting to live through than to contemplate, as Maria herself discovered, for in later years she was never able to recall it without a yawn. It was only on the most painful experiences in her life that she looked back with any interest, whereas her months with Sarah resembled a calm sea, the dullest of all ideas. Variety was decidedly lacking. It would be true to say that the history of one day would be the history of the whole period, so we might as well have the history of that day, chosen not quite at random. The one I have in mind came towards the end of the idyll, and was quite eventful, in its quiet way.

We join Maria in Regent's Park. It was her habit on days which, like this one, were not too busy, to walk into the park to eat her lunch and to escape, for a while, the bustle of the office. She would find a vacant bench in one of the most secluded parts of the park and sit there for nearly an hour, sometimes thinking, sometimes looking around her, sometimes dozing and sometimes feeding the birds. For this last purpose she would bring with her a paper bag full of stale crumbs. Today she also had a packet of sandwiches, egg and cress, bought at a take-away in Baker Street. These turned out to be disgusting. She ended up eating the stale crumbs and throwing the sandwiches to the birds. That soon got rid of them. Alone, Maria closed her eyes and listened to the sounds around her. It sometimes surprised her to realize that she very rarely listened to the world, and that she was seldom in any useful sense conscious of the noises of footsteps, traffic, voices, the wind, so that lately she had taken a resolution to pay more attention to this aspect of things. It was a way of emptying her head, too, of all the scraps of conversation, real and imagined, and of music, remembered and invented, with which she was otherwise plagued night and day. It was a long time since Maria had heard silence, real silence, and it would be a long time before she heard it again. But she was not averse to the sound of Regent's Park at lunchtime. It was a winter's day, sunny but essentially cold, and the park was not busy. She could hear two men talking in Japanese, and a baby crying, and a woman saying, There, there, presumably to the baby, and the cooing of hungry pigeons, and the shouts and laughter of distant children. At the back of all this was the loud hum of the city going about its business.

Maria was in a good mood. She did not enjoy her work and was not looking forward to going back to it that afternoon, but her distaste for the job usually comprehended nothing more serious than boredom, and she recognized with periodically recurring amazement that in all other respects she had hit upon a way of life which rather seemed to suit her. She liked living with Sarah. She got on passably well with her other flatmate, Dorothy. And she was even beginning to like London, for those very things which she had believed would make her hate it, for its bruising impersonality, for the anonymity which it afforded her, for the fact that she could pass through it unthought of, uncared for, unthreatened. She preferred to be at the mercy of the places in which she lived, to feel that she meant nothing to them. All her life she had, it was starting to seem, been at the mercy of forces beyond her control, so perhaps she had come to feel comfortable that way. This does not mean that Maria accepted no responsibility for her own actions. She knew, for instance, that there had once been a moment at which she had been presented with a choice as to whether or not to marry Martin, and she knew that she had made that choice too quickly and too carelessly. All the same, it seemed to her that chance had not played entirely fair. How was she to know that her fiancé would turn out to be, at the end of the day, and to be perfectly frank, and when all was said and done, a malignant shit, not to put too fine a point on it? And was it her fault that the choice had to be made at a time when she was alone, unhappy, and quite without a direction in life? It was too easy to get bitter, though, and besides, Maria never sulked, especially on sunny winter afternoons. She was also rather shocked to have found herself using the phrase 'direction in life', like one who had lost her wits. The only direction in her life led south-west out of the park into Baker Street, and she would have to follow it in about ten minutes, she knew that perfectly well. After that there would be a new direction, due north towards Hornsey, and so it would go on, turn and turn about, until she lost the use of her legs, or the inclination to use them, whichever was the sooner. Another fifty years or so. This partial statement of the case appeared to please her, for she smiled, and an old woman who happened to be passing, thinking that the smile was directed at her, smiled back. What presumption, and yet Maria didn't resent it, so amiable was her temperament when the circumstances were in her favour, so indiscriminately philanthropic was her disposition when life was being just a tiny bit decent to her. As a girl she had been quite lovable, would you believe. Memories of her childhood, her cheerful, pampered childhood, dripped back into her mind that afternoon. She did her best to keep them out. How her parents had loved her, how happy they had been in those days. Maria usually fought against ideas like this. Therefore she rarely went home to visit her parents, for she found it painful to compare their present state of lonely contentment with the sustained and infectious moods of joy which she knew she had once inspired in them, even when she was being an ungrateful little brat which was, on reflection, most of the time. Edward had never inspired joy like that in her, although she had always assumed that he would, one day.

Basically families were a mystery to Maria. Her brother represented the only aspect of that life with which she was still at all in sympathy. And this was one reason why she had invited him to dinner that evening.

Pensive, but not yet gloomy, she made her way back to the office. Maria worked, as I said, in Baker Street, in the offices of a women's magazine. Her job was to look after the photograph library. Whenever somebody wanted an illustration for an article, whether it was the publicity still of a famous actor or a full colour photograph of the steak and kidney pudding featured in that week's recipe, she had to provide it, either from the enormous box files which filled the basement in untidy stacks, or, if no suitable picture was to be found there, from some agency which could supply one or arrange for a new picture to be taken. Someone with a greater sense of humour would have found it easier to take this job seriously. As it was Maria simply thought it silly and dull, and put as little energy into it as possible, her approach in fact frequently verging on the absent-minded, for it was not rare for her to supply a picture of a steak and kidney pudding in place of that of a famous actor, and vice versa. These fits of abstraction prompted her colleagues to coin a nickname, 'Moody Mary', a fact which might have amused Maria, had she been able to remember that that was what they had called her at school, and had she been endowed with a greater sense of humour. Instead it gave her a certain amount of private annoyance. It would be no more than the truth to say that Maria did not like her colleagues, and it would scarcely be false to say that Maria's colleagues did not like Maria. Not that a perfectly healthy working relationship cannot be maintained between colleagues who dislike or even hate each other, of course, but it would be stretching things to say that Maria's working relationship with her colleagues was healthy.

Let us not exaggerate here, though. Besides, first of all we must describe these colleagues, attempt a little bit of characterization for a change. The first surprising thing about Maria's colleagues is that most of them were men. Yes, although this magazine addressed itself to an audience of women, on subjects such as were thought to fall exclusively within the woman's experience, it was written and edited almost entirely by men, although some of them adopted assumed, female, names for this purpose. Take, for instance, its leading story writer, a man called Barry, who had previously earned his living as a chartered surveyor but who now wrote romantic serials under the pseudonym Nesta Vypers. His latest effort, *The Heart Will Walk*, told the affecting narrative of a young ballet dancer who, after being crippled in a road accident, gradually falls in love with the motorist who has run her down, then miraculously recovers the use of her legs when he at last kisses her at the end of a long romantic push around Hyde Park, and promptly marries him with a cavalier disregard for his appalling track record of wrecked marriages and motoring offences. Barry and Maria had been on frosty terms ever since she had described this story, in an unguarded moment, and upon being pressed for an opinion, as a load of old cock. (In her years away from Oxford she had not lost all her critical faculties.) Among the other writers was one called Lionel. He edited the agony column, offering his readers advice on problems marital, domestic, romantic, personal and sexual. The title of his column was 'Chastity Wise – a Shoulder to Cry On', and this was a typical exchange:

Dear Chastity, My husband and I have been happily married for five years, until last week. Every Sunday at lunchtime he goes down to the pub and drinks nine pints of Guinness with his friends from the Rotary Club, while I stay at home and do the roast. His favourite is beef with carrots and mash. This week they were all out of carrots so I gave him parsnips instead. When he saw there were no carrots he called me a filthy name, threw his dinner in my face and them emptied the whole of the gravy boat all down my dress. I have never known him like this before. Please tell me what to do as I am at my wit's end.

Dear Worried, There is no easy way to remove gravy stains. You should handwash the garment in hot water and if ordinary powder doesn't work, try using some white spirit. As for the long-term problem, why not keep a stock of carrots handy in the deep freeze?

These, then, were the two thorns in Maria's flesh. Not that they ever came to blows, or even that an atmosphere of unbearable mutual animosity was created, or even that they treated her much worse than the other people in the office did, or they did the other people in the office. No, Maria was merely subjected to a stream of little discourtesies, a string of subtle signs of disrespect, recognizable but barely definable as such. For instance, whenever she passed Barry in a corridor, or on the stairs, she would smile at him, not because she associated the presence of Barry with emotions which made her want to smile, rather the opposite, but because when you pass someone on the stairs like this, it is customary to give some token of recognition. Now Barry would invariably smile back, but not in the same way. His smiles were sudden and rapid acts of aggression. He would direct his face towards Maria, allow a brittle grin to flash across it for perhaps half a second, and then resume his former expression before turning away, so that her last view was of his angry mask. It was his way of reminding her that he was quite capable, where she was concerned, of perverting such polite conventions to his own ends without, technically, violating them. What mystified Maria was his readiness to perform this tiny ritual of personal aggrandisement several times a day, day in, day out, all year round, whenever, in fact, chance determined that their paths should cross. But, as you know, Maria was generally not unhappy during this period, so she did not let it bother her much, any more than she let Lionel bother her. Lionel had a penchant which was still more amusing. His delight, whenever he and Maria approached a door together, was to hold the door open without looking behind him, as if out of habit, and then to glance back at the last moment, see who it was for whom he was holding the door, and let it fall shut in her face. Pleasant variations could be performed on this routine, on those not infrequent occasions when he would be passing through a doorway in the company of another woman, with Maria bringing up the rear. He would ostentatiously hurry ahead and hold the door open, standing aside to admit the woman, who might be either the magazine's general editor or the girl who opened the post and made the coffee, it didn't matter, and then he would let it shut just as Maria, fully aware of her mistake, would be attempting to come through it. Sometimes, if he was in a particularly sparkling humour, he would even give the door a little kick with his heel, in order to impart extra velocity. Maria, who had more than once had a carefully arranged pile of photographs knocked out of her hands and thrown into disarray by these means, could frame no plausible explanation for Lionel's behaviour and thus found herself unable either to resent or to condemn it.

After work that evening, Maria did not go directly home. She had some shopping to do. She took the tube to Archway, and then caught a bus up Highgate Hill. She had left a little early, with permission, and arrived just as the shops were starting to close. By now she was feeling quite extraordinarily cheerful. London at dusk from the top of a bus had seemed strange, homely and entrancing, at first by turns and subsequently all at once. She had almost forgotten to get off. Now she clutched Sarah's shopping list and hurried from shop to shop. The most important things were the vegetables, but there was also the meat, of course, and they were low on flour and last night when they were planning the meal they had been unable to find any basil, although both could have sworn that they had some. In fifteen minutes it was all done and she started making for home.

Seated around the table that evening, counting clockwise, and starting with Maria's brother, who sat at the head, were Bobby, Dorothy, Ronny, Maria, William and Sarah. Of these only William, if I remember rightly, has not been mentioned before. He was a friend of Sarah's, in fact that is putting it midly, he was a close friend of Sarah's, so close that all their colleagues at work, which was where they had met, confidently expected an engagement to be announced in the near future. Sarah and Maria both thought that this was very funny, and loved to joke about it together. They think we're going to get married, Sarah would say, laughing. How absurd, Maria would say, shaking with mirth. They just can't understand, Sarah would say, with a smile, that in this day and age it's quite possible for a woman and a man to see a lot of each other, even to love each other, without there being anything romantic or sexual in it at all. Blinkered isn't the word,

Maria would say. She and Sarah understood each other very well, in those days.

By the time the first course was served, a little idle conversation had taken place and it had become clear that by a happy coincidence the spirits of all those present were good. They embarked with enthusiasm on a light helping of fettucine, tossed in cream and butter, sprinkled with freshly grated parmesan and spiced with a little nutmeg, and served with a medium dry Italian white which did much to enhance the already festive atmosphere.

'It's moments like this,' said Bobby, 'that make everything worthwhile. I sit at my desk all day, in an overheated office, poring over figures and looking at the clock, and I think to myself, Robert, what's the point of it all. Then I come here, and in a few minutes life seems worth living again. Good wine, good company, good food . . .'

'Wonderful food,' said William.

'Delicious,' said Ronny.

'You could go to a restaurant,' said William, 'and pay fifteen pounds, and the food wouldn't be nearly so good as this.'

'Fifteen pounds?' said Ronny. 'Fifteen, did you say? I was in a restaurant last week and it cost me twenty-five pounds. Twenty-five! The food was cold, the meat was tough, the greens were off and the cream was sour. There's nothing to beat a home-cooked meal.'

'Twenty-five pounds is nothing,' said Bobby. 'I paid

forty-two pounds for a meal last Friday and it never even came! Two and a half hours I waited at the table and they didn't even bring me a starter. And even if they had, it wouldn't have been as good as this because this couldn't be better. Happy any man,' he concluded, 'whose wife could cook him such a beautiful meal.'

'Hear hear,' said Ronny.

'Rather,' said William.

'When are you going to get married then, Robert?' Dorothy asked, shortly after the arrival of the second course. It comprised sautéed veal scaloppine with marsala, and two side dishes, namely zucchini fried in flour and water batter and, which was a special treat, gratinéed Jerusalem artichokes. They accompanied it with a rather expensive Soave.

'I'm not sure that I ever want to get married,' said Bobby. 'After all, I think it would be true to say, that everybody seated around this table has serious reservations about marriage, of one sort or another, yes?'

'Yes,' said Dorothy.

'Reservations,' said Bobby, 'based on close observation and rational thinking.'

'Or personal experience,' said Dorothy, with a sidelong glance to her left. Subtlety was not one of her virtues.

'"Marriage has many pains, but celibacy has no pleasures,"' quoted Sarah, coming to her friend's defence. 'Isn't there something in that?'

'Johnson lived in a less enlightened age,' somebody said.

'How ironic, then,' said somebody else, 'that it should have been called the Age of Enlightenment.'

'I wonder what age we are living in now.'

'This is the age of consent.'

Everybody laughed, including the speaker, but they had after all been drinking for nearly an hour. Dorothy, who had her mouth full at the time, spilled food all over the tablecloth. Sophistication, like subtlety, was not one of her virtues.

Maria now served a large bowl of fruit, apples, pears, bananas, grapes, nectarines, mango, cantaloupe and apricots, soaked overnight in orange and lemon juice and flavoured with maraschino liqueur. There was enough for everyone to have two helpings. Silence gradually took the place of conversation, as it began to dawn on them all that they had consumed an amount of food that was, to be honest, grotesque. Each, independently, was seized with a sudden desire never to get out of their chairs again for the rest of their lives.

'That's the lot,' said Ronny, emptying the last droplets of wine into Maria's glass.

'No more wine?' said Sarah sleepily, her head lolling against William's shoulder.

Maria happened to know that Dorothy had another bottle of red in her bedroom, but didn't ask her to get it, for she also knew that generosity, like sophistication and subtlety, was not one of her virtues.

Bobby and Maria went into the kitchen to make coffee.

They sat at the table and talked while waiting for the kettle to boil.

'Well, Bobby, it sounds as though you are doing all right at last.'

'What makes you say that?'

'Well, you must be earning a penny or two to be able to afford restaurants which charge forty-two pounds.'

'Oh, that. Yes.' But finally he confessed, 'Maria, I'm in trouble again. I've run out of money, and the bank are starting to lean hard on me.'

Maria tutted.

'I'm not lending you any more money. I have enough trouble keeping this place up without giving it all away to my brother. And you know that you never pay it back.'

'Is that your last word, then?' Bobby asked.

'Yes.'

They relapsed into a sullen silence, which was soon interrupted by the entrance of Dorothy.

'Come to do the washing up?' Maria asked.

'Bog off,' said Dorothy. (Delicacy, like generosity, sophistication and subtlety, was not one of her virtues.) 'I want a glass of water.'

'Maria,' said Bobby, when she had gone, 'do you remember that night in Oxford, when I was staying with you? And I went out at night, and didn't come back till four in the morning?'

'Of course I remember.'

'Did you ever wonder where I'd been?'

'Of course I wondered. You know I did. Why?'

'Well, if you were to lend me a little money – just fifty pounds, that's all – then I might tell you what happened.'

Maria wrote her brother a cheque, but as soon as he had folded it and put it away in a pocket, she knew that she had been tricked.

'I'll tell you when I've cashed it,' he said. 'Honestly. I promise.'

He left the kitchen just as Ronny was coming in. He had come to slip in a quick proposal of marriage before going home. Maria refused, more kindly than she had used to do, and when she showed him out, she kissed him goodbye.

Bobby and William left together, since they lived in the same part of London. There was more kissing, both formal and tender. Dorothy was not in on this, having fallen into a drunken stupor on her bed, after making successive and fruitless passes at all three men, on the pretext of asking them into her bedroom to mend her alarm clock. Virtue was not one of her virtues.

That left Maria and Sarah, alone in front of the fire, as so often before.

'What a lovely evening,' said Sarah.

Maria had no grounds for disagreement.

'What a beautiful day it's been.'

This, on the other hand, seemed slightly too rhapsodic. All she would concede was, 'Yes, I quite enjoyed it.'

'Today,' said Sarah slowly, 'has been the happiest day of my life so far.'

Maria looked at her in surprise. 'Really?'

'Yes.' She smiled at her friend's astonishment. 'Can you not guess why?'

Maria said nothing.

'While you were in the kitchen, with Robert, and while Dorothy was in her bedroom, with Ronny, I was in here, with William. He proposed to me.' She stood up. 'We're going to be married.'

8. A Great Day for Ronny

Spring that year was rainy. Maria rarely had the inclination so much as to step outside, whether to go for walks or to visit friends or to see plays or films. Instead she would sit on her bed, staring blankly at the drizzle and waiting for the time to pass. Many, many weekends were spent like this. She could hear Dorothy occupying herself in the other rooms, busy with guests, or records, or the television, or some other form of amusement. Very occasionally Maria would join her, and they would exchange broken sentences, but more often she would wait until Dorothy had gone out before venturing into another part of the flat, for it no longer made sense to pretend that they liked each other very much. To be fair to Dorothy, Maria was not a very likeable person under these circumstances, and to be fair to Maria, Maria realized this full well, but found herself for weeks unable to break out of a state of cold languor, a mood of wearied acceptance of whatever garbage life elected to throw at her. In the office they stopped using the nickname Moody Mary, as betokening too much affection, and instead began to consider ways of getting rid of her.

There was, in fact, another reason, besides Maria's general disagreeableness, for the deterioration of her relations with her flatmate. This was that Dorothy, tired, I suppose, of going to bed with a succession of different men, and charmed, no doubt, by Maria's physical attractions which, in case I didn't mention it before, have, throughout this book, been considerable, although I won't go into details, impressed, I repeat, desperately trying to pull the threads together, coming to the point at last, by these, she attempted to seduce her.

The mouths of my male readers have perhaps begun to water at the imminent prospect of a titillating tableau. I'm sorry, for their sakes, to have to say that this will not be forthcoming. Dorothy's approach was extremely direct (sophistication, subtlety, etc., not being, etc., as explained in the previous chapter), and, so much the better for me, exclusively verbal. She introduced the subject one evening in early April, a bright, wet evening on which for some reason or other Maria chose not to retire to her bedroom immediately after dinner, but to sit quietly on the sofa, gazing with tired eyes in the general direction of her own feet. Dorothy was reading a magazine, but her heart obviously wasn't in it, for she laid it down after flicking through its pages for a few minutes in an attitude of signalled carelessness.

'Heigh ho,' she said (and if you believe that then you will, I rejoice to think, believe anything), 'time passes slowly sometimes, doesn't it?'

Maria nodded, faintly.

'Do you miss Sarah, Maria?'

'Yes, I do, sometimes.'

'Poor Maria,' said Dorothy, with a pitying smile, and sounding more like Charlotte every minute. 'I feel for you. Life is so empty for you now. I wish there were more sparkle in your life.'

'I'm all right,' said Maria, contemplating retreat.

'You don't have a lover, do you, Maria?'

'No.'

'Not even someone whom you would like to love? Not even a glint in your eye?'

Maria apparently did not consider this question worth answering.

'I have a glint in my eye, though.'

Maria looked up, and found that this was indeed true. She began to feel slightly uncomfortable.

'I'm surprised you don't have a boy friend, Maria. You're very beautiful.' The preliminaries were over, and Dorothy came straight to the point. 'Maria, let's go to bed now, and make love.'

Maria raised an eyebrow.

'Are you serious?'

'Of course I'm serious. Let's explore each other's bodies, there's nothing on the television.'

'Thank you, I'd rather not.'

Appalled as she was by the proposition, Maria did not yet move. She was interested to hear the explanation for this new development in Dorothy's behaviour.

'But why not?' said Dorothy.

'Because I'm not attracted to you. You're a woman.'

'Oh Maria, how can you be so narrow-minded! Where's

your sense of adventure? I'm asking you to travel with me, to reaches of physical pleasure where no man can take us. I'm asking you to demonstrate the independence of our sex. We might achieve an ecstasy we've never felt before, and at the very worst we'll have made a valid political statement. Where's your self-respect? I want to lead you down a sexual avenue which it's every woman's duty to explore. Why won't you come with me?'

Maria had been about to say, 'Because it's a cul-de-sac', but changed it to, 'Because of the No Entry signs', which I think you will agree is wittier and is, in fact, the only recorded instance of her ever having made a humorous remark. It annoyed Dorothy no end. She took the magazine and threw it across the room in a gesture of disgust.

'It's no wonder you're lonely, Maria. It's no wonder everybody hates you.'

With that she ran into her bedroom and slammed the door. Maria sat pondering her last words.

One consequence of this incident was that Maria took a resolution which had long been brewing. She decided that it was time to find a third person to share the flat. She and Dorothy had agreed, when Sarah had first moved out to live with her husband, that they should only attempt to find a new tenant if it should become financially imperative. That time, Maria felt, was fast approaching, but she now also felt a need simply for further companionship. Why I say 'simply' I don't know, because such needs, common to all but a happy few, are far from simple, and the possible ways of satisfying them are even less so. But

Maria seems to have assumed, with flaccid and, it must be said, entirely uncharacteristic optimism, that it would be feasible to find a replacement with whom friendly or at least pleasant relations might be enjoyed. She had perhaps in mind a woman of about her own age (Maria is now twenty-nine). However, Dorothy had other ideas.

'Well, I don't see why we shouldn't try to find someone,' she conceded, when Maria suggested it to her over breakfast the next morning. 'But I don't think we should advertise. We don't want to take anybody who might happen to come in off the streets. Did you have anyone in mind?'

'No.'

'None of your friends? But I forgot, you have so few friends. Well, you'll just have to let me think about it, and we'll see what can be done.'

That evening Dorothy returned from work in a mood of excitement.

'I've found just the person, Maria,' she said.

'Who is she?'

'His name's Albert. You wouldn't mind that he's a man, would you?'

'Not if he's nice. How did you meet him?'

'At work.'

'Is he a new colleague?'

'No, he's a patient.'

Dorothy, I should inform you, worked at a hospice for recovering alcoholics.

'A patient? What makes you think he'd be suitable?'

'Maria, he told me his whole story today. It's pitiful. The tears were streaming from my eyes, you never heard anything so tragic. He's absolutely homeless and hasn't got a friend in the world. He only ever to took to drink because he had nobody to love him or care for him. You've never seen such a poor lonely old man.'

'Old? How old?'

'He's seventy-four.'

'Dorothy, this isn't a hospital. It's not a geriatric unit. It's a flat. It's a home.'

'Maria, don't be so heartless. A home is exactly what he needs.'

'Well, I think it sounds a horrible idea. I'm sorry I even suggested finding someone. I warn you, I shall be furious if you try to bring that man in here.'

The words came with difficulty to her lips, for fury was in fact an emotion of which she was no longer capable, and to compound the problem she was a poor actress. Nevertheless, she believed that she had made her position clear, and that Dorothy would respect it. In this she was mistaken. For, arriving home rather late from work the next day, she was immediately struck, upon opening the front door, by a peculiar smell. It was hard to define exactly, but years later, searching for words in which to describe it, Maria said that it was almost as if a small herd of cattle had arrived, reeking of whiskey, and used the sitting room as a latrine. A grizzled old man, dressed awkwardly in new, ill-fitting clothes, was sitting on the sofa drinking from a mug of tea. He stood up when she entered, introduced himself as Albert, told Maria that she must be Maria, and said how much he liked his new room. Maria went to find Dorothy and they had a short, inconclusive argument. Maria then lay on her bed for the rest of the evening. She felt a slow chill steal over her.

A week passed. During this time her initially vague but insistent unease began to assume a more definite shape. She was soon able to classify her objections to the presence of Albert under the following four headings: smell, drink, flatulence, and other. As for the first three, it was quite likely, she realized, that they existed in some relationship of complex interdependence which she was not equipped to understand. Dorothy had of course assured her that he had forsworn alcohol for the remainder of his natural life, but this assurance seemed to be at odds with various circumstances, such as the fact that on the second morning of his residence, Maria, in attempting to leave her bedroom at seven thirty, had found herself unable to open the door, the obstruction, it transpired, being Albert's prostrate body, which had fallen there several hours earlier on its way to the bathroom, intending no doubt to relieve itself of the rum with which it had been privately regaling itself all evening. This incident, which Dorothy laughingly brushed off as a 'relapse', turned out to be the first in a series.

Furthermore, Albert did not take easily to everyday domestic life. His attempts to use the vacuum cleaner resulted more often in the breakage of fragile objects, such as small items of china, or chairs, than in any noticeable improvement in the appearance of the carpet. When trying to use the shower he flooded the bathroom. He could not cook. He disliked Maria, or so his terms of reference would seem to imply, for he was heard to describe her as a 'miserable slag'. He very rarely spoke to her directly at all, although this may have been for want of opportunity, since her excursions from her bedroom became increasingly infrequent. On the other hand he appeared to like Dorothy, whom he affectionately called 'Dotty', and he would willingly execute small commissions for her, little tasks which she imposed on him as a manifestation of her trust. For instance, she would give him sixty pounds, and ask him to go to the supermarket and do the week's shopping for the three of them, barely uttering a word of reproach when he returned after half an hour with a loaf of bread, a pork pie, and seven bottles of gin. These were the sorts of minor failings, marginal errors of judgment owing as much to inexperience as to anything else, which Maria classified as 'other'.

By the end of the first week, she knew that she was going to have to find somewhere else to live. It crossed her mind more than once, as it has conceivably the reader's, that this was precisely the outcome that Dorothy, mortified by the failure of her recent advances, had intended to provoke, and that no sooner would Maria have packed her bags and gone than Albert himself would be quietly booted out and left to resume his former life.

But she realized that to charge Dorothy with this intention would only be to invite further wide-eyed accusations of cruelty and cynicism. So she found herself in a tricky situation, and not for the first time. Weighed down by unhappiness, and bored with always having to keep it to herself, she thought that it might alleviate the problem a little to talk about it with someone, a friend, say, supposing one could be found. Idly she flicked through her address book. There were three entries, under B for Bobby, R for Ronny, and S for Sarah. She remembered that it would be no use trying her brother, because he had gone back to visit her parents for the weekend. What about Ronny? She smiled, none too cheerfully, as she recalled another time, nearly eight years ago, when she had surprised herself by choosing to visit him at a moment of crisis. A fat lot of good that had done her. But he had changed since then, and so had Maria, and although he was still as silly as ever about wanting to marry her, she no longer felt uncomfortable with him, in fact quite the reverse, for there was something about the very familiarity, amounting even to predictability, of his behaviour, which inspired in her a real and otherwise unavailable sense of comfort. She decided there and then, with a thrill of pleasure, to phone him. They had not seen each other since the night of the dinner party. How surprised he would be to hear from her!

But there was no answer. So Maria phoned Sarah, and they arranged to meet for dinner that evening. Sarah nominated a restaurant in Hampstead.

She looked slightly more plump and pale than when Maria had last seen her, on the day of her wedding. As usual, they kissed before sitting down together, but it was only Maria who did so with any fervour.

'Well, this is nice,' said Sarah, unnecessarily.

Maria smiled.

'It was nice to hear from you. It was a very nice surprise.'

'I just wanted to see you, that's all.' Maria paused, then asked:

'How do I look, Sarah?'

'You look very nice. And very well,' said Sarah, staring fixedly at her fillet of sole while waiting for the tartare sauce to come.

'No, how do I really look. You weren't looking at me.'

Thus prompted, Sarah examined Maria with some attention.

'Actually you don't look too well. I'd noticed already, but I didn't think it would be polite to say so.'

'I don't want you to be polite. I want you to be my friend.'

'Why, Maria? Is anything the matter?'

'I'm unhappy. I think I'm going to move out of the flat. Only I don't know where to go, or what to do.'

A tear fell from the corner of Maria's eye. Fortunately the waiter, who arrived at that moment with the tartare sauce, had his handkerchief with him and was able to wipe her cheek.

'Thank you,' said Maria, feeling very stupid.

'We must remember to give him an extra tip,' said Sarah, when he had gone, and added earnestly: 'Maria, you must tell me everything. You must tell me all about what's gone wrong. You have my undivided attention. Can I have your lemon if you're not going to use it?'

First of all Maria told her about Dorothy's attempted seduction. Sarah was shocked and a little embarrassed. She blushed.

'That does surprise me,' she said. 'Still, one always finds problems with shared accommodation. Don't misunderstand me, Maria, I enjoyed living with you and Dorothy very much. But it doesn't really bear comparison with having your own home, and sharing it with the man you love. Living with friends, by which I mean girl friends, of course, is all very well while you're still young and you haven't found your place in the word, but it can never really be as nice as married life. I don't want to give you a lecture, Maria, just because I happen to have the benefit of more experience than you, but you can have no notion of how lovely it is to share everything with the man you love, a bed, your food, your money, your home, all your thoughts and experiences, your whole life, in fact.' A thought now struck her, and she laid down her knife and fork. 'But I was forgetting, you've been married already.'

'Yes.'

'I'm sorry, Maria. How thoughtless I'm being. Of course, it doesn't always work out as well as it has for me. How is little Edward?'

'I never see him. I thought you knew that.'

There was a long and frosty silence. Finally Maria, determined to retrieve something constructive from her friend's sentimental outburst, but feeling, at the same time, less and less sympathetic and interested, asked coldly:

'So you think that marriage is probably the answer to all my problems, and everybody's else's.'

'It's not quite as simple as that, of course, Maria,' Sarah answered, with a sweet smile. '"Marriage has many pains, but celibacy has no pleasures", as somebody once said. I don't want to generalize, because that would mean nothing to you. I can only speak out of my own experience, and over the last few months I've known such happiness . . .' She paused and reflected. 'It's not enough, you see, Maria, just to be friendly with someone. You'll never get deep into life like that. There must be intimacy, close, personal and physical intimacy. To share a meal with someone, for instance. I mean, here we are, sharing a meal together, at least, we would be – ' she looked around angrily in the direction of the kitchens ' – if they'd hurry up and bring us the next course. Honestly, I'm ravenous. Anyway, here we are, sharing a meal, but there's no real *intimacy* in it, do you see what I mean? It's not like sitting down to a meal with your husband, a meal which you've cooked yourself, and watching him eat it, watching him watch you eat, talking all the time with your eyes. Do you see what I mean?'

Maria considered her own recollections of married mealtimes.

'But when you hear the sound of food in his mouth,' she said, 'don't you feel like stabbing him with the carving knife?'

Sarah, thinking that she was joking, smiled.

'Of course not.'

'Is there nothing about him that you find repulsive? What about when you're having sex?'

'Maria!'

'Whenever I saw Martin naked, I always wanted to chop it off. I'd never seen anything so grotesque.'

'Don't be silly. There's nothing ugly about . . .' here her voice sank very low '. . . men's privates. You're embittered, Maria, and you forget, because it was all such a long time ago. You've forgotten what it was like.'

This was far from the truth, for Maria had not forgotten, and never would forget, about penises. She had had them up the front, round the back, down the hatch, and dangled in front of her nose, and was rather hoping that she would never have to see one again in her life. But she didn't bother to say so to Sarah.

'Did you never love Martin, Maria?'

She shrugged. 'As you say, it was all such a long time ago . . .'

'Have you ever been in love at all? Ever?'

She laughed. 'You asked me the same question once before. But that was even longer ago.'

'But have you, Maria? Have you ever been in love?'

'No,' she answered, since even heroines tell lies occasionally. And she knew that it was a lie even as she said it, because she was thinking of a day in Oxford, the day of the storm, when she had waited for so long in the dreadful heat, and Fanny had told her that a man had rung. The noises of the restaurant died away and for a moment she could only hear the clatter of her feet on the stairs as she ran up to her room to cry.

Then she noticed that Sarah had leant forward and was holding her hand. She withdrew it.

'Anyway,' she said, 'what's the use of talking about marriage if I haven't even got anyone to marry.'

'Well,' said Sarah, 'there's Ronny.'

This actually made Maria laugh. 'Now who's being silly!'

'I'm not being silly. You say you haven't got anyone to marry. But look how often Ronny's asked you.'

'Yes, and look how often I've refused him. I'm very fond of Ronny, you know. Very fond. But that will never happen.'

'Why not?'

'Oh, I don't know.' Maria sighed, and pushed her plate away. 'I've got other plans, I suppose.'

'Oh? Such as?'

'Nothing definite, as yet. I'm tired of London, Sarah. I think I might give up my job, and leave. I know it's not easy to get jobs any more, but I've got to get away from here. I don't know where I'll go, yet. I thought that just to start with I might go back to live at home, with my parents. It's so long since I've seen them properly, I feel I hardly know them any more. Bobby tells me they still keep my old room for me, just as it used to be. It would be nice to go back there for a while.'

'You can't live in the past, Maria.'

'Oh, I know that. My past is nothing to write home about, anyway. But I've got to start again, from somewhere.'

In fact the idea of returning home had only occurred to Maria that evening. Somehow she had started to feel weak and foolish in front of Sarah, and all she had been trying to do was to put up a feeble pretence of resolve. Having presented herself with this new option, however, she thought carefully about it on the bus back to Hornsey, and came, eventually, to the conclusion that it probably wouldn't do. It was only as a small child that she had ever enjoyed living at home, and there was no reason to suppose now that she and her parents could co-exist happily together. Sarah had been right to be sceptical. The whole evening, it now seemed, had been wasted, for it had not helped her to reach a decision, and had only shown that she and her best friend no longer understood one another. Maria's heart as she unlocked the door of the flat was heavier than ever.

Although it was late, Dorothy was waiting up for her. Maria could tell immediately from her agitation that she had some bad news.

'Your mother phoned,' she said. 'You must phone back at once. She left this number.'

Maria did not recognize the number, but it was her mother who answered. Her voice was breathless and tearful.

'Where are you?' Maria asked. 'Why aren't you at home?'

'I'm next door, at Mrs Chivers'. Oh Maria, there's been a terrible accident. It's all Bobby's fault. He was staying in your room, because you know it's the one we always keep nice, and he came down late to watch the football, and he must have left his cigarette burning, and oh my darling, half of our house is in ruins, it's been burnt down to a cinder.'

Maria found words, at this juncture, to be of no use to her.

'All your bedroom, and all your lovely things, and all your wardrobe, and everything, and your desk with all your old school books, it's all gone, and it spread to the bathroom, and downstairs.'

'Is anyone hurt? Are you all all right?'

'Yes, we're all still here, thank the Lord our God. We could so easily have been killed, all of us. But everybody escaped. Everybody. Except – '

'Yes?' Maria suddenly tightened her grip on the receiver.

'Except Sefton.'

There was a moment of deathly silence, and then Maria dropped the receiver, threw herself onto the sofa, and wept until she was too tired to weep any more.

*

This time Ronny answered on the second ring. It was Sunday morning, breezy but bright and with every prospect of a fine sunny afternoon. Maria told him what had happened, explained that Bobby was looking after her parents and that there was nothing to be gained from her going home, and asked whether he was free to spend the day with her. Of course, the answer was yes, she had expected no other. Ronny had once told her that he would, if necessary, have cancelled an audience with the Queen if it coincided with an appointment to see Maria, and she remembered this remark, about the funniest he had ever made, believe it or not, with a grateful smile as she watched out of her bedroom window for the sight of his car.

They drove aimlessly out of London, bearing, did they but know it, slightly to the north-east. Neither spoke much, Maria for obvious reasons and Ronny, I suppose, because as usual he had nothing to say, although today Maria fancied that she could sense a deeper reticence, deriving perhaps from his sympathy over all that had lately befallen her. They were a silent, sombre pair, then, by the time they arrived in Broxbourne, where they decided to stop for lunch. They ordered one meal and shared it between them, so small were their appetites. In the afternoon they walked beside the river. The sun, as promised, was shining in a half-hearted way, but at four o'clock it abruptly disappeared behind a screen of grey, a breeze began to blow, and Ronny insisted that Maria wear his jacket, which he had been carrying over his shoulder all afternoon. Fearing rain, they took shelter in a roadside café and ordered two cups of coffee.

'Have you enjoyed this afternoon?' Maria asked.

'Yes, it's been lovely,' said Ronny. 'It's so nice to get away from the city, and to be with you.'

'You've been very quiet,' she said.

'There's a certain sort of silence, Maria,' he answered quietly, 'where no words are necessary, and which signals not the end but the start of understanding.'

Maria stared at him in surprise, trying to recall when she had heard those words before.

'Yes, I suppose there is.'

It was now, she felt, merely a question of waiting. She stirred her coffee, slowly, deliberately, with the plastic spoon provided, and this in spite of the fact that she did not take sugar, thinking to herself with amusement meanwhile of all the other times when she had sat in silence with Ronny awaiting, dreading, the inevitable question. Should she have agreed long ago? No, she thought not. What did it matter now, anyway.

'Well, I think we'd better be getting along, don't you?' said Ronny suddenly, looking at his watch. Then, noticing that Maria seemed shocked: 'I'm sorry, you haven't even finished your drink. Don't let me rush you.'

'It's not that.'

He seemed not to understand.

'It's just that . . . there's something that you normally do, Ronny, which you haven't done today.'

'Oh?'

She could not even bring herself to be exasperated, so excited was she that the moment was about to come, even if it had to be forced.

'You haven't asked me to marry you,' she said.

Ronny gave a good-natured laugh.

'It's not like you to tease me, Maria, but it shows you're feeling better, so I can't be angry with you.'

'But why?' she asked. 'Why haven't you?'

'Because I know you'd say no. Maria, I've been asking you that question for nearly ten years now, and I may be a bit slow, but even I start to realize in the end when I'm fighting a losing battle. You've been very patient with me. I know you've always seen me as a friend, and I've always wanted to be more than that. Well, you've got enough troubles, without me making a nuisance of myself. I see that now. So you don't have to worry, Maria. That's all over.'

'But today,' she said, 'I wanted you to ask me.' She took a last good look at his far from handsome face, his foolish, questioning mouth, his absurd ears, and felt a little quiver of doubt, but she brushed it aside. 'Because I was going to say yes.'

I feel in no position to describe the reaction which this statement produced. Visually, it was complex. It was also absolutely silent.

'Ronny, will you marry me?'

There was a short pause, in which it is impossible to say whether he was hesitating, or deliberating, or recovering from his astonishment, or whatever.

'Yes,' he said. 'Of course. Yes.'

★

It rained heavily on the day of the wedding. Maria had made all the arrangements. She had wanted it to be done as quickly as possible, and as quietly as possible. She had not wanted her parents to be present, although it proved necessary to take Bobby into her confidence. As soon as he returned to London, she contacted him, told him of her plans, and then moved all her belongings out of the flat and into his spare bedroom, where she was to stay for the next few days. She handed in her resignation at work, and managed to book a time at a London register office for the end of the week.

'I don't want anybody to be there except you,' she said. 'I just want the whole thing to be over with, and done. It's just like going to the doctor's or the dentist or something. There's to be no ceremony and no fuss.'

Having heard and agreed to this, Bobby was surprised to enter his sister's bedroom on the morning of the great day and to find her trying on a hat, in front of the mirror. It was a small hat, red and pretty. She seemed embarrassed.

'I don't know,' she said, 'I was walking past the shop yesterday afternoon, and just thought that it looked nice. After all, I thought that I ought to do something a bit special. It's not every day of the week that a girl gets married.'

They took a taxi to the register office, arrived early,

and sheltered from the rain in the doorway of an adjacent shop while waiting for Ronny to appear. Maria put on her hat, and admired her own reflection in the shop window against a background of magazines and sex aids.

At five past eleven she looked at her watch and said, 'He's late.'

But Ronny was more than late, and after half an hour the truth of the matter was obvious. The bastard had stood her up.

Maria and Bobby crossed the road and went into the local fast-food restaurant. They were the only customers. They took a window seat, drank tea, and, between them, tried to decide what she should do next.

9. *Maria in Exile*

Three years later, and it is still raining. I tell a lie, of course, there have been intervening periods of sunshine, but they do not concern us. To find Maria now, you would have to travel far to the north, for she lives in Chester. A fine city, I fully recommend that you visit it one day. A Thursday in autumn, for instance, would be ideal. This, on the other hand, is a Tuesday in summer, and yet it is still raining, but there you are, that's England for you. Maria is walking home from work, and we find her, you'll be pleased to hear, in an interesting frame of mind. Not that she is actually doing anything special, to all outward appearances, but then we would have had to choose our moment very carefully, very carefully indeed, in order to catch Maria doing anything special, during her time in Chester. If her happier days in London resembled a calm sea, then her days in Chester resembled a desert. An infelicitous figure, that, though, because it fails to take account of the rain. What I am really trying to say, as you can hardly fail to be aware, is that life for Maria was, at this stage, extremely dull, and by dull I do not just mean that nothing of interest ever happened, although it didn't, but that it was a life lived in a dulled state of mind, seen and felt through a perhaps irreparably dulled consciousness.

Well, I know how she feels, I have unhappy memories of Chester myself, but it cannot be the fault of the place, surely, because look at all those fine old buildings, and that splendid cathedral. Maria was especially fond of the cathedral, which is strange, because she was not naturally of a religious temperament. It was one of her few pleasures, nevertheless, to go into the cathedral on light summer evenings, when it would be full of visitors, many of them in attitudes of prayer, to kneel down beside one of them, and then, if she was feeling passionate, to hurl abuse at her creator, or, if she was feeling calm, to present him with reasoned and fully substantiated accusations of professional incompetence. All this was done in silence, of course, so as not to disturb her fellow-worshippers. Maria, whose nature was essentially trusting, had always believed in God, but on the other hand she saw no evidence whatsoever that he believed in her. She frequented the cathedral like a ghost, and its grounds too, for she spent many evenings, and some afternoons, in the Garden of Remembrance, a shady spot which actually has not much going for it other than its name. What an opportunity for metaphor! Unfortunately we don't have the time. There is a bench there, with its back to the cathedral wall, where you might often have seen Maria sitting, apparently deep in thought, or lost in wistful recollection, or sunk in romantic yearning, but in reality her mind a complete blank, unless she was wondering whether to have ravioli or tortellini for her supper that night. Many were the evenings, and many the afternoons, when lonely young men would stop to gaze at her with eyes full of longing, or would sit down beside her and engage her in suggestive conversation, or would sexually assault her while nobody was looking. Even here, among the dead, Maria could not guarantee that she would be left alone, which was now all that she desired, all that she asked of the world. Of course, never in her life having been left truly alone, she was in no position to know whether that was what she truly wanted, so, since accuracy seems to be the order of the day, it would be better to say, no doubt, that all that Maria wanted was the chance to find out whether being left alone suited her. Nothing else did, after all.

But she lives alone in any case, you protest, or would do, if I had told you that she lives alone, and if I haven't I must say it's because I thought that any intelligent reader would have guessed as much by now. Yes, Maria lived alone, and was therefore free to enjoy as much solitude as she could wish, one would have thought. And yet this was very far from being the case. Sheer perversity, surely. The explanation, quite a simple one I assure you, is that Maria never felt less alone than when she was by herself, in her own house. It was her own self which she most wanted to escape. Sounds rather trite, put like that, doesn't it. We must recognize, though, that included in what Maria, or was it me, termed her self, was a whole crowd of people who really had no business to be there at all. I don't have to remind you of their names, for you know them all; I have introduced all the important ones in the course of telling this story. These people, former friends, former husbands, former colleagues, brothers and mothers and fathers and sons, simply would not leave Maria alone, and never more so than when she was alone in every other respect. Their voices and faces and sometimes bodies filled her thoughts, dominated her feelings and dulled each and every one of her senses. They had become so thoroughly attached to her self that she was obliged to cart them about with her wherever she went, even though they weighed a ton, and nothing would have pleased her more than to be able to dump them on the wayside.

It was in the hope of shaking them off that she had come to Chester. Why Chester, you ask? It is true that she chose the city more or less at random, but it had one factor heavily in its favour, which was that neither she, nor anyone she had ever known, had any former connection with it whatsoever. You see, in her simplicity, Maria had resolved to start a new life. She seems to have believed that if she could only remove herself geographically from all the people and places she wished to leave behind, then they would cease to exist. Or at least, if she did not actually believe this, and I must admit that it seems unlikely, she thought that it was at any rate worth a try. This will give you some idea of how distraught she was at the time. She certainly hadn't banked on them all coming with her, and installing themselves like so many phantoms in her home and in her mind.

But see how many guns I am jumping, talking about

Maria's home when I have not even explained where or what it was. Maria lived, then, in a large terraced house, in a row of other large terraced houses, not far from the football ground. The house had three floors, and a total of eight rooms, only five of which she ever used. As for the others, she could have let them out to lodgers, if she had liked, if she wanted the company, say, or if she needed the money, but she neither wanted the company nor needed the money. Her job was well paid. She worked in a women's refuge, a small cluster of houses on a quiet side of the city, whose exact location was kept a close secret. Here women who had been forced to leave their husbands because of cruelty, violence, or any of the other by-products of married life, could come and take cover for a while, with their children if necessary, and could then afford to feel relatively safe from the threat of pursuit and recapture. You should not assume from this, incidentally, that Maria had suddenly developed a social conscience. On the contrary, she found her work dispiriting and unrewarding. She had applied for the job because it was advertised, and she had accepted it because she was offered it, it was really as basic as that. She had been glad of it at first, partly because it gave her something to think about other than the past, and partly because she was tired of not having enough money to live on. When she first arrived in Chester, she had had no money at all, apart from a small sum which she had saved in London, which was just enough to cover the deposit on her new house.

Here, then, she lived alone. She did not even want to

keep a cat any more. All those old ways had been discarded, as having proved ineffective. She no longer listened to music, in the dead of night, with her eyes fixed on the red light of the cassette recorder. She preferred instead to go to sleep at once, sleep now being one of the very few aspects of existence for which she felt any degree of enthusiasm, except that occasionally she would find herself dreaming, and nothing browned Maria off so much as that. She would awake feeling intensely cheated. There are two kinds of dream, are there not, the good and the bad, a misleading classification if ever there was one. Maria did not know which she detested more. Dreams, as you know, are no sooner described than falsified, so it would be pointless to go into details, but the bad were those which brought her out in a sweat of fear and revulsion, and from which she awoke feeling even more drained than when she had gone to sleep, and the good were those which filled her with waves of hope and with a nameless quietude, and from which she would awake to the plunging realization that these delightful sensations had been, after all, no more than visionary. So it was much better not to dream at all, from her point of view. And there was this consolation, at least, that sleep came fairly easily to Maria at this period. I see no reason to add insomnia to her list of torments. She would often have to suffer only as few as five minutes of consciousness before dropping off altogether, and in the event of luck not being on her side on any particular night, she had devised a clever series of mental exercises which were as good as an anaesthetic. She would attempt to remember, in alphabetical order, the names of twenty-six different diseases of the body, all beginning with a different letter, and she had never yet to her knowledge had to go beyond gastro-enteritis. This game was open to endless variation, and for diseases she would sometimes substitute towns, vegetables, poets, breeds of dog, varieties of apple, colours, famous footballers, schools of philosophic and critical thought, musical instruments, surgical instruments, film directors (although N was a stumbling block in that one, she found), rivers, modes of transport, classical deities, fish, religious sects of the seventeenth century, or anything else she could think of. It would be a bad night indeed, then, on which she could not manage to keep thoughts of the past out of her head for the time it took to fall into an exhausted stupor. A very bad night. And yet it happened, more than once. Conversations, voices, would come hammering at her door, crying to be admitted. And how often, during those wakeful seconds, did she hear the words: a man rang. I can't remember. Did he give his name, no. Did he leave a message, no. No.

Which did Maria enjoy less, the weekdays, or the weekends? Difficult to answer. Weekends were lonelier, because at work she would talk to her colleagues, and to the inmates of the refuge, usually because she had to, and now and then because she felt like it, whereas at the weekend she would talk to nobody, unless to the young men who molested her in the cathedral grounds, or to the girls on the till in the supermarket where she did her week's shopping. And she would talk to herself, too, just to keep her hand in. There seemed little point in losing the faculty of speech merely for want of practice, she never knew when it might come in useful again. As she stood in the queue at the supermarket, for example, soft cries might escape Maria's lips, gentle words of protestation, such as 'Sod this for a fucking bitch of a life', or 'Puke and shit, puke and shit, day in, day out'. As a result of making these remarks, Maria would get funny looks. And while on this subject I think it would be true to say that Maria was generally unpopular in her neighbourhood, and tended to be regarded with a suspicion which spilled over, for some people, into violent hatred. She never gave any offence, knowingly, but her neighbours mistrusted her because she lived alone, and was silent, and because the sight of her walking home from work on wet nights, huddled with cold, wearing a plastic headscarf to guard against the rain, somehow depressed them. But perhaps I can see their point, I feel depressed just writing about it.

And now is there anything more, I wonder, that you can possibly want to know about Maria's years in Chester. Did she ever leave the city, for a holiday, or for a seaside outing? No, never. Did she not communicate with her family, all this time? Very occasionally, by letter, or by telephone. Did she never have any visitors to stay, in the spare bedroom, none of those old friends who thronged her fancy in moods of fond remembrance? Unnecessary sarcasm. No, of course not. Then surely I have told you all that you need to be told. Yet looking back, it seems to be rather a short chapter. Well, there is next to no direct speech, so you are still getting value for money, of sorts. Let's be honest, I begin to weary of Maria, and her story, just as Maria begins to weary of Maria, and her story. What little fun there ever was in her, and in it, seems to have quite gone away, and I wouldn't be at all surprised to learn that she desires nothing more than to have it brought to an end, rapid and painless. Let us move on, for I have only one more episode to relate of Maria's life, and then we shall be done, and we can say goodbye.

But there, you start chatting with the reader and before you know where you are you find that you have forgotten all about narrative. Did I not say, at the beginning of the chapter, that it was a Tuesday, and that there was something particularly interesting about Maria's thoughts, as she walked home from work? Something had happened that day, you see. Something which had stirred up, in Maria, emotions which had lain dormant, unfelt, unattended to, for many years. A new woman had come to the refuge, with her child. The boy was nine years old, they were fleeing from a husband who had attacked and beaten them in a drunken rage, and Maria had recognized them at once as Angela, her old nanny, and her son, Edward.

10. *Afterhand*

It is one week later. Some impulse, it would seem, for she still has such things, has brought Maria to an unaccustomed place, viz. Chester railway station. It is Saturday morning. The weather? My, what sticklers for detail you are. Distinctly cloudy, with the possibility of light showers. She looks around her, at the scenes of coming, and going, and waiting, mainly the latter. The platform is not busy. She stands close to the railway line and looks both to the right and to the left, not knowing where the train will be coming from. Maria is southbound this morning. She is going home. Don't ask me what has brought this on, but having made up her mind she is rather looking forward to it, to seeing her family again, after all these years. Perhaps it will all turn out to be a miserable disappointment, but no, I don't think so, this time. She has a good excuse for going back, in that she has been invited, and a small celebration is scheduled to take place in honour of her father, who will be sixty years old tomorrow. What could be nicer, how could one conceive a more fitting way of their honouring the occasion, than for the four of them to sit around the dinner table for Sunday lunch amidst the ruins of their old dining room? Only joking, the house has been substantially rebuilt by now. But it will be pleasant, she thinks, just this once, to try not to forget the past, but to recreate it, and thereby, perhaps, to come to terms with it. Worth a try, at any rate.

Do you mind if we revert to the past tense? I find the other so exhausting.

Something about the quiet bustle of the station, even though it was not busy, seemed to please her. She found herself watching the activities of the porters with something approaching interest, and the feeling with which she regarded the other passengers almost amounted to curiosity. She wondered, idly enough to be sure, but how else can you do it, who they were, and where they were going, and why they were going there, whether any of them had upon their hands a journey as important as Maria's journey was for her, a final return after long absence. None of these other travellers, I might add, paid the slightest attention to Maria, whose heart was reaching out to them so warmly. They would have found her curiosity impertinent, and her attempts at sympathy uncalled for. For we all have our daily business to get on with, even on Saturdays, and there are times, and there are places, the railway station being one of them, at which we prefer the recognition of our interdependence to be kept to a minimum. A few words to the person who sells you your ticket, a nod to the person who punches it on your way to the platform, and that will do nicely, thank you. Not that Maria had any design, Heaven forbid, to enter into conversation with any of the strangers in whose company she was obliged to travel that morning.

Nevertheless she had a strange sense, an absolutely unaccountable and unpardonable sense, that she was being ignored. This sense persisted until her train arrived, and she had found herself a comfortable and secluded seat on it.

Just as the train was pulling out of the station, a young woman clambered aboard. She made her way breathlessly through Maria's compartment, with no apparent intention of taking a seat in it, but as she was walking past Maria herself, the train gave a lurch and the woman fell into her lap. They laughed and apologized, and the consequence was that the woman decided to sit opposite Maria after all. Maria took the opportunity to allay a small anxiety.

'Is this train direct?' she asked. 'Or do we have to change?'

'You change,' the woman said. 'You change at Crewe.'

'Thank you. I've never done this journey before.'

'I do it all the time,' said the woman. 'Do you not live in Chester?'

'Yes, I do. I just don't travel by train very often.'

'Well, of course, you have a point. Cars are so much easier. And cheaper, too, if there's more than one of you, if you want to take the family anywhere, or something.'

'I don't have a family. I'm not married,' said Maria.

She must have sounded ashamed, for the woman appeared to be trying to reassure her when she said, 'Never mind, neither am I.'

'Do you live alone?' Maria asked.

'Yes. I've tried other ways, but, well, in the end, I thought I'd rather be by myself. At least it means there's only one person around to get on my nerves. My name's Mary, by the way.'

'Oh. I'm Maria.'

'Almost the same.'

They both laughed.

'I thought,' Maria began, 'I was beginning to think I must be the only woman in the world who lived alone.'

'Oh, no, you'd be surprised. There are quite a lot of us, hiding away in the woodwork. People who've realized that you can get a lot more done if you don't have to spend half your time darning someone else's clothes and doing the ironing.'

'You like living alone, then?'

'Yes, I do. I have my freedom. That's everything, isn't it?'

'I suppose so,' said Maria, but she could not stop herself from asking, a few seconds later, 'Freedom to do what, though?'

Mary shrugged, confused by the question.

'To do whatever you like, of course,' she said. 'Why, is that not how you find it?'

'I don't know,' said Maria, 'I sometimes feel that in the last few years I've achieved less than ever. But then I'm not sure I ever did achieve anything. I'm not sure I know what it means. I brought someone into the world once, a little boy, but that's about it.' She smiled, a quick, rueful smile, and repeated, 'That's about it.'

'You mustn't be so negative,' Mary said, earnestly. 'Just look around you. Look how beautiful the world is.' The train was entering Crewe at the time, so she had not chosen her moment well. 'Think of all the wonderful opportunities that might be just around the corner. Think of all the love and happiness in the world.'

Maria had a brief go at this, and then said, 'Could you be a little more specific?'

'What makes *me* happy, do you mean?'

'Yes, if you like.'

'Well, that's easy. I suppose the thing that makes me most happy in all the world is being with my boyfriend.'

'Your boyfriend?'

'Yes. He's got a job in Stoke, you see, and I work in Chester, so every weekend I go over and stay with him. It gives me something to look forward to all through the week. Of course, it's not as if we can't talk to each other in between, on the telephone. I should say that either he phones me or I phone him at least every other night. But we think it's important to have separate jobs, and to be independent.'

'Independent, yes, I see what you mean.'

'It's what we women have been fighting for, after all, isn't it? And now I'm able to have my cake and eat it, you see, because I can get up to all sorts of things in Chester and he doesn't have to know about them. I mean, I wouldn't like you to think I'm promiscuous or anything, but it's not as if we're married, and I do love Keith, he's terribly sweet and everything, but after all you're only young once and I don't see why I shouldn't have a bit of fun, while the sun shines, so to speak. That's the real advantage of living alone, don't you find?'

Maria nodded, without, it must be said, much conviction.

'Take last night, for instance. Normally I go to Stoke on Friday night but yesterday there was this party so I decided to stay for it. I phoned Keith to tell him, of course, and he didn't mind a bit. We just have that kind of relationship. We're a very modern couple. Anyway, I'll tell you what happened at the party. Well, there I was, dancing away to the music, you know, the way you do, and suddenly this man came up and grabbed me by the shoulder. He was a bit rough with me but terribly goodlooking and so we got talking, and before long he was saying the rudest things to me, you can't imagine. Do you know what he called me?'

Maria did not know what he had called her.

'He called me "a proper bit of tit, fit for nothing but to be fucked till I dropped". Well, naturally I couldn't help being flattered in spite of myself – '

But at this point Mary's anecdote was interrupted by a cry of 'All change!', and they realized that the train had stopped.

'Well, here we are. The parting of the ways,' she said. 'It's been so interesting talking to you. I'm afraid you'll just have to imagine what happened next. It was amazing, simply amazing. Have a good weekend, won't you. Where did you say you were going?'

This conversation provided much food for thought on the remainder of Maria's journey. The thought which it fed was not exactly new, but she was aware that today it impressed itself upon her with a greater energy than usual. Her old unthinking torpor gave way, as the train headed south, to a flux of questions whose importance she had always sensed but which she had never dared actually to put to herself before. And even as she considered them, she was made to recognize, both her reason and her intuition pointed out to her, in the kindest possible way, that they could never be answered, never, never be answered now, and so even these questions gave way, in the course of time, to a different preoccupation, namely, a slow and growing awareness of familiarity with the landscape into which she was being carried. A familiarity based not on the sighting of particular landmarks, but on her feeling that the very contours of the hills and fields, and the very shapes and colours of the buildings, now appeared as surviving monuments to the existence of a much earlier self whom she had long forgotten. She knew, of course, that they could not bring that self back to life, perish the thought, but they reminded her of it in a way which she did not find disagreeable. These were Maria's impressions, as the train at last drew into the station, and deposited her in the city of her birth.

It was by now lunch time, and she was feeling hungry. But the station buffet, new décor notwithstanding, looked as unattractive as ever, and besides, she had had a happier thought. She would have something to eat at the old café at the bottom of the hill. So she walked into the city centre, and waited for a bus.

The bus took her past her old school, St Jude's, which she realized she had not seen since the day she left it, fifteen years ago. She had a vague recollection of the day she had sat in Mrs Leadbetter's office, receiving the headmistress's congratulations, but it was not at all vivid, dark winter evenings being hard to visualize on summer Saturday afternoons. One detail, however, bobbed up in her mind quite distinctly, and she sighed. *Per ardua*, maybe.

Her plans for lunch were thwarted, because when she reached the terminus she found that the café no longer existed, if it ever had. The petrol station which used to stand adjacent to it had been extended, in order to provide car-wash facilities, and presumably the café had been demolished to make this possible. Maria was not in the least upset, you understand, she was not one to stand in the way of progress, but she could have handled a sandwich, less for old times' sake than for the more pressing reason that she hadn't eaten since eight o'clock in the morning. The thought of the long walk uphill on an empty stomach did not appeal to her. She could have phoned home for a lift, it is true, but she didn't. Nothing seemed to have changed much, a few trees felled here, a new house there. Indeed, Maria did not notice the most significant change of all, which is that it took her ten minutes longer to walk up the hill than it had used to. Finally her parents' house came into view, doing its best to look as it had always done, and Maria walked up the old drive, hesitated, and rang the doorbell.

I see no need to describe the ensuing scenes, in fact it would be difficult to do so with accuracy. No, we shall move on, leaving out about twenty-four hours, and rejoin Maria's family around the dining table at half past one on Sunday afternoon. They had drunk sherry in the sitting room, and now they were having a bottle of wine, not very good wine, Maria thought, with their meal, for days like this do not come often. Bobby carved the joint, and Maria served the potatoes and sprouts, while their parents smiled and watched intently, pleased apparently with the novelty of being waited on. Then they all started to eat. Maria had forgotten how seriously her family took their meals. They were perfectly single-minded about it, and although she at first made occasional attempts at conversation, remarking, for instance, on her mother's excellence at cooking, even though it had been Maria herself who had done most to prepare the meal, her comments were never answered, and neither of her parents uttered a word until their plates were empty. Even Bobby, who, you will recall, had been so talkative over his food in Chapter Seven, solemnly observed the family tradition, but then he was more used to it, perhaps it didn't seem so strange to him. It was her father who at last broke the silence.

'Not a bad joint of beef, that,' he said, laying his knife and fork neatly together on the plate. 'Very nicely done, too. Potatoes were a bit soft.'

Bobby noticed that his father's glass was nearly empty, and poured him some more wine.

'Let's drink a toast,' Bobby suggested. They all gripped their glasses expectantly. 'To Dad,' he said. 'Happy birthday.'

'Happy birthday.'

'Well,' said their father, 'isn't it funny how time marches on. Sixty years on, and it doesn't seem a day since you two were little kids.'

People always say things like this on their sixtieth birthday.

'It isn't sixty years since we were little kids,' Bobby pointed out.

'You know what I mean,' his father said. 'Days like this, they make you think.'

'I bought you a birthday present,' Maria said.

From a drawer in the sideboard she fetched a small packet. It was oblong in shape, and had been wrapped in red wrapping paper. It was found to contain a gold wristwatch.

'It's a watch,' said her father, examining it with delight. 'And it's got my name on the back.'

'I had it engraved.'

He kissed her warmly.

'I'm touched, Maria. I'm deeply touched. More than that, I'm moved. I'm deeply moved. What a wonderful present for a man to get from his daughter, on his sixtieth birthday. To think that you still care, after all this time.'

'And it's not just decorative,' said his wife. 'It's practical.'

'Exactly. Of course it is. Of course it's practical. I've only got to look at this watch, and not only shall I think of my daughter, but I shall know what time it is.'

'I'll go and fetch the pudding,' Maria said. 'Bobby, will you help me clear away?'

She had hoped, I think, by descending into practicalities to put a stop to her father's maudlin ramblings before it was too late. But it was already too late. Barely audible above the noise of shifting crockery, he continued to drone on about the strangeness of time's passage, forgetting, apparently, that things would be very much stranger if time did not pass at all, and he was still at it when Maria served him his bowl of apple pie and custard.

'It's funny, isn't it,' he said, taking an enormous mouthful which in no way seemed to impair his speech. 'I can even remember my own father's sixtieth birthday. I can remember him looking and feeling exactly as I do now.' He sighed. 'Eight years later he was in his grave. I'll never forget that day. We sat around their old table, and we drank, and laughed, as if we hadn't got a care in the world.'

'What, the day he died?' asked Bobby.

'Not the day he died. I'm talking about his sixtieth birthday. Can't you listen, for a change?' He turned to Maria, and his tone softened. 'Do you remember that day?'

'No.'

'You were only three. Oh, but he was fond of you, Grandad was. He used to take you on his knee and bounce you up and down, almost until you were sick sometimes. He loved his little Maria. You were the delight of his old age, you two were. His grandchildren.' He picked up his glass, but found that it was empty. 'Of course, your mother and I haven't been so lucky, when it comes to grandchildren.'

Maria and Bobby looked at one another. Their mother coughed.

'They'd only make you feel old,' Bobby said.

'You'd only get tired of them making a mess and a noise all over the place,' said Maria.

'That's for me to decide,' he answered, and looked darkly at Bobby. 'It's about time you got married, if you ask me. You can't gad about chasing women all your life.'

'I don't chase women,' said Bobby.

There was a short silence, to allow time for the rest of the family to realize that this was true.

'More pie, anyone?' Maria then said, hurriedly.

'I think we all ought to do something this afternoon,' said her mother, as more helpings were distributed. 'You know, the whole family. We ought to go somewhere together. Just like in the old days.'

'Where to?' asked Bobby, without enthusiasm.

'Yes, where to?' asked his father, likewise.

'Let's go to the park,' said Maria.

'The where?'

'You know, the park. Where you used to take us when we were children.'

'I don't remember any park. There's no park near here.'

'Yes you do,' said Maria's mother. 'Up on the hill, not far from the motorway.'

'Oh, that,' he said. 'Yes, I remember that. What do you want to go there for?'

He gave his grudging agreement at the time, but when, an hour later, Maria asked him if he was ready to go, he cried off altogether. The City match is on television in a minute, he said, and besides, I'm getting a bit old to go climbing up hills. A bit old, said Maria, listen to you. A few grey hairs and you start acting as though you've lost the use of your legs. Don't you make fun of my grey hairs, he said, you're not short of a few of those yourself, and he wasn't lying. Am I not allowed to do what I like on my own sixtieth birthday? Yes, father, of course you are, Maria had answered.

If your father's not going, her mother said, I think I'll stay here with him. They were in the kitchen. I'm going to bake a cake, she said, a birthday cake for his birthday tea. And some scones. I don't fancy climbing that great hill in this heat. Why don't you and Bobby take the car and go by yourselves, you could have a lovely walk together. All right, said Maria, we will.

Bobby was sitting in the garden, under the shade of the sumac tree, out of the sun. Maria brought him a glass of lemonade, with ice, and one for herself, and then sat down on the grass beside his deck chair.

'Are you coming to the park with me?' she asked.

'Wouldn't you rather go by yourself?'

This conversation takes place slowly, by the way. Don't rush it.

'Not really. I'm tired of doing things by myself.'

'No, I think I'll stay here. I've had a lot to eat, and I feel sleepy.'

Maria sipped her drink, disappointed.

'What did you mean just now,' she asked, 'when he told you that it was about time you got married, and you said – '

Bobby's laugh interrupted her, quiet though it was.

'You love to build up mysteries around me, don't you? Do you remember that time in Oxford? When I went out to get something to eat, and didn't come back till the morning?'

'Now you're going to tease me again.'

Bobby smiled. 'Only because I think you like it.' He touched her with his foot.

'Yes,' said Maria. 'Yes, I do like it.'

And so it transpired, as we might all have guessed, that Maria drove to the country park alone. She drove in her father's car, with the radio tuned to Radio Three. It was a broadcast of Prokofiev's F minor violin sonata, always one of her favourites. At the end of the first movement, its quiescent harmonies and wandering melody seemed especially in keeping with her own thoughts. She turned into the car park at the foot of the hill and found it almost empty. The sky was a cloudless blue. She locked the car and began to climb.

On her way to the summit the sound of the wind was,

at first, the only sound of which she took any notice. Then she started to hear others, the distant cars, the songs of birds, the cries of children. 'Cathy! Cathy!', a child was calling, thus:

But there were very few people on top of the hill, that afternoon. Two men were playing with a model aeroplane, and an old couple were walking their dog. Otherwise Maria, and the birds, and the cows, had the place to themselves.

She passed by a huge electric pylon which she remembered well, and then found herself at the very crown. Here some thoughtful person, paid no doubt to do such things, had erected a toposcope. There will be those among you to whom the word means nothing, probably, so I should explain that this is a kind of round map, carved in stone. What a gift for explication. It informed her, much to her interest, that the towns of Stafford and Lichfield lay due north, Coventry and Rugby due east, Cheltenham and Gloucester due south, and Ludlow due west. This will incidentally enable the curious to reconstruct her position with some accuracy. She turned her gaze, for the time being, to the east, but all that she could see were the tower blocks of outer Birmingham in a blue haze, and, prominent among them, the green-tipped tower of Rubery asylum. She tried to calculate how long it had been since she had last seen that view.

Maria had come to this hill for a specific purpose, and an unashamedly nostalgic one. She had hoped that it would remind her of the day when a small girl, whose name had been Maria, it now seemed, by no more than coincidence, had come there with her family, and had lost them, and had cried and fallen into the long grass. And indeed it could hardly do other than to remind her, or at least to make her think of it, but the recollection was regrettably pale, on the whole. The countryside around her called attention to itself, rather than to the memory of that long-lost other afternoon. While she wandered around, then, in a vague search for the exact spot where she had fallen, she could not help being distracted by the colours of the gorse, the rustle of holly bushes in the wind, the sight of a jay darting before her, by hawthorn. Hawthorn. Her mother had once taught her to sing, A little bit of bread and no cheese, like the chaffinch. What was that doing in her mind, all these years on? She felt suddenly and savagely sad to have seen her parents looking so old. But even this moment passed, and in its wake Maria felt, now, a curious lack of emotion. All at once the park appeared to have nothing to do with her memory, it belonged neither to her youth nor to her middle age, neither to remembrance nor to hope, and this was good, because from now on Maria would be leaving all of these things behind.

She could hear a lark singing nearby. The bird was

perched on a branch of the hawthorn bush, and was looking at Maria with intense interest, fascination, you might say. She returned its stare, and for a while these two creatures stood quite still, watching one another. I find the thoughts of both, at this point, equally impossible to divine. It is even hard to say with which, of the two, I feel more in sympathy, but let us for the sake of this story cast our lot with the lark, for whom the sight of Maria's quick unmoving eyes eventually became too much. He flew off the branch and launched himself into mid air. On the ascent, he took another look at her, saw her dwindle, spiralled, saw her move, saw her smaller and smaller still, climbed, looked again, saw her little figure on the hillside, climbed higher, and higher again, and then saw only the hillside, where we must leave her, leave her to her last calm, Maria, a speck in the unseen, homeward bound, alone, and indifferent, indifferent even in the face of death which who knows may be the next thing chance has in store for her.

By the same author

A TOUCH OF LOVE

Robin, a postgraduate student in Coventry, has spent four and a half years not writing his thesis. Now he hides in his room, increasingly frightened of the world around him. His friends have failed him, and love eludes him. His only outlet is his short stories, scribbled in notebooks, which express his secret obsessions and frustrations.

Then, when an unfortunate incident in a public park lands him in serious trouble, his life spirals out of control. It seems that nothing, in life and fiction, turns out as predicted ...

'Magnetic ... a moving tale' *Observer*

He just wanted a decent book to read ...

Not too much to ask, is it? It was in 1935 when Allen Lane, Managing Director of Bodley Head Publishers, stood on a platform at Exeter railway station looking for something good to read on his journey back to London. His choice was limited to popular magazines and poor-quality paperbacks – the same choice faced every day by the vast majority of readers, few of whom could afford hardbacks. Lane's disappointment and subsequent anger at the range of books generally available led him to found a company – and change the world.

'We believed in the existence in this country of a vast reading public for intelligent books at a low price, and staked everything on it'
Sir Allen Lane, 1902–1970, founder of Penguin Books

The quality paperback had arrived – and not just in bookshops. Lane was adamant that his Penguins should appear in chain stores and tobacconists, and should cost no more than a packet of cigarettes.

Reading habits (and cigarette prices) have changed since 1935, but Penguin still believes in publishing the best books for everybody to enjoy. We still believe that good design costs no more than bad design, and we still believe that quality books published passionately and responsibly make the world a better place.

So wherever you see the little bird – whether it's on a piece of prize-winning literary fiction or a celebrity autobiography, political tour de force or historical masterpiece, a serial-killer thriller, reference book, world classic or a piece of pure escapism – you can bet that it represents the very best that the genre has to offer.

Whatever you like to read – trust Penguin.